CW01511083

HULL LIBRARIES

5 4072 10280207 5

KINGSTON UPON HULL
CITY LIBRARIES

THE FLAT IN NOTTING HILL

Love and lust in the city that never sleeps!

Izzy, Tori and Poppy are living the London dream—
sharing a big flat in Notting Hill, they have good
jobs, wild nights out…and each other.

They couldn't be more different, but one thing is for
sure: when they start falling in love they're going to
be very glad they've got such good friends around to
help them survive the rollercoaster…!

THE MORNING AFTER THE NIGHT BEFORE
by Nikki Logan

SLEEPING WITH THE SOLDIER
by Charlotte Phillips

YOUR BED OR MINE?
by Joss Wood

ENEMIES WITH BENEFITS
by Louisa George

Don't miss this fabulous new continuity from
Modern Tempted™!

Dear Reader

When I was invited to participate in a continuity series for the Modern Tempted™ line I was absolutely thrilled, and when I found out who my co-writing partners in crime were I knew we were in for a fun and very special time. I'm a huge fan of authors Nikki Logan, Joss Wood and Charlotte Phillips, so creating characters and stories with them was a real treat.

The Flat in Notting Hill series follows four couples—eight very busy people—living, working and falling in love in London. For my couple, Poppy and Isaac, that means living and occasionally working *together* whilst ignoring the attraction between them that has been simmering for years!

Poppy made a big mistake a long time ago and has been trying to make amends ever since—with the consequence of not fully living her life. Isaac, on the other hand, with his own demons to conquer, has grabbed life by the horns and thoroughly made his mark by being very successful in his business life but not so much in his personal one. It takes one night of them being left alone together in the flat for the tensions to come simmering to the surface and for them to take a step into unknown and very uncertain territory.

It was such fun to write about a cast of characters who have become family to each other over the years, and to steer Poppy and Isaac along towards the future they both deserve—even though they're very reluctant from the outset! And setting a book in London is always great for me as it brings back wonderful memories of living there (in a flat in Notting Hill too!).

I hope you enjoy Poppy and Isaac's story. This is book four in the series, so if you want to find out what happens to Izzy and Harry, Alex and Lara, and Tori and Matt their books are THE MORNING AFTER THE NIGHT BEFORE, SLEEPING WITH THE SOLDIER and YOUR BED OR MINE? I know you'll love their stories too.

For all my writing and release news visit me at www.louisageorge.com

Louisa x

ENEMIES WITH BENEFITS

BY
LOUISA GEORGE

All rights reserved including the right of reproduction in whole or in part in any form. This edition is published by arrangement with Harlequin Books S.A.

This is a work of fiction. Names, characters, places, locations and incidents are purely fictional and bear no relationship to any real life individuals, living or dead, or to any actual places, business establishments, locations, events or incidents. Any resemblance is entirely coincidental.

This book is sold subject to the condition that it shall not, by way of trade or otherwise, be lent, resold, hired out or otherwise circulated without the prior consent of the publisher in any form of binding or cover other than that in which it is published and without a similar condition including this condition being imposed on the subsequent purchaser.

® and TM are trademarks owned and used by the trademark owner and/or its licensee. Trademarks marked with ® are registered with the United Kingdom Patent Office and/or the Office for Harmonisation in the Internal Market and in other countries.

First published in Great Britain 2014
by Mills & Boon, an imprint of Harlequin (UK) Limited,
Eton House, 18-24 Paradise Road, Richmond, Surrey, TW9 1SR

© 2014 Harlequin Books S.A.

Special thanks and acknowledgement are given to Louisa George for her contribution to *The Flat in Notting Hill* series.

ISBN: 978-0-263-24331-4

Harlequin (UK) Limited's policy is to use papers that are natural, renewable and recyclable products and made from wood grown in sustainable forests. The logging and manufacturing processes conform to the legal environmental regulations of the country of origin.

Printed and bound in Great Britain
by CPI Antony Rowe, Chippenham, Wiltshire

Having tried a variety of careers in retail, marketing and nursing (where a scratchy starched uniform was mandatory), **Louisa George** is now thrilled that her dream job of writing for Mills & Boon® means she gets to go to work in her pyjamas.

Originally from Yorkshire, England, Louisa now lives in Auckland, New Zealand, with her husband, two sports-mad teenage sons and two male cats. Writing romance is her opportunity to covertly inject a hefty dose of pink into her heavily testosterone-dominated household.

When she's not writing or reading Louisa loves to spend time with her family and friends, enjoys travelling, and adores eating great food (preferably cooked by someone else). She's also hopelessly addicted to Zumba®.

Visit her at www.louisageorge.com

Other Modern Tempted™ titles by Louisa George:

HER CLIENT FROM HELL
BACKSTAGE WITH HER EX

**This and other titles by Louisa George
are available in eBook format
from www.millsandboon.co.uk**

DEDICATION

To Nikki Logan, Joss Wood and Charlotte Phillips—
thanks so much for the fun and the friendship
during the creation of this wonderful apartment and
the people in it. It was an absolute pleasure working
with you all—I hope we can do it again some time.

To #TeamKISS for help with the cocktail names—
many thanks to you all! I hope we all get to have
a Merry Margarita together one day!

This book is dedicated to my fabulous editor Flo Nicoll.
Thank you for your continued support,
help and advice—you are amazing!

CHAPTER ONE

1st December. Operation Christmas

CHRISTMAS MUSIC. CHECK.

Dodgy Christmas tree and decorations from attic. Check.

Decent bottle of red and one extra-large glass. Check... *Oops*...one bottle down. Better make that two bottles of decent red...

Poppy Spencer dumped the years-old artificial tree by the corner window and started to pull back its balding branches, creating a kind of...sort of battered tree shape.

It was about time someone in this apartment got into the Christmas spirit and if that meant she had to do it on her own, then she would. So what if her AWOL flatmates were too busy to care about the festive season? She had to do something to fill the long, empty holiday that stretched ahead of her.

'Never mind, poor thing.' She was talking to a tree? That was what being alone in a flat, which until recently had resembled a very busy Piccadilly Station, did to a reasonably sane woman. 'Looks like it's just you and me. We'll soon have you shipshape and looking pretty and sparkly for when everyone comes home. Cheers.'

She chinked a branch with her glass and took a large

gulp. There were few things in life that beat a good Shiraz. It went down rather quickly, coating her throat with the taste of blackberries and…well, wine. She poured another. 'And here's to absent friends.' All of them. And there appeared to be more going absent every day.

The box of baubles and decorations seemed to have ended up in a similar state to the tree: a nibbled corner, depilated tinsel. Mice perhaps? Surely not rats? She shuddered, controlling the panicky feeling in her tummy… Rats were horrific, nightmare-inducing, disease-ridden rodents and mice their evil little siblings.

So maybe she wasn't alone after all.

Standing still, she held her breath and listened. No telltale scurrying, no squeaks. Quiet. The flat was never quiet. Ever.

Oh, and there was some woman crooning about not wanting a lot for Christmas. Yeah, right, said no woman ever.

Note to self: ask big brother, Alex, to look for evidence of four-legged friends—the man had fought in Afghanistan; he was more than equipped to deal with a little mouse infestation.

Second note to self: Unfortunately, Alex was sunning himself on an exotic beach somewhere with Lara. And Isaac, the only other male flatmate, was…well, hell, who ever knew where Isaac was? He was like a sneaky, irritating nocturnal magician, here one minute, gone the next, probably expanding his über-trendy bar portfolio along with his list of short-term female conquests.

Tori had gone with Matt to South Africa. Izzy had moved in with Harry. That was it, all her friends out, happy, settled. Doing things with significant others—or, in Isaac's case, insignificant others.

Was it too much to want a little bit of their collective happiness? Someone to care if she died alone, suffocated under a box of musty decorations or knocked out by a toppling balding Christmas tree, toes nibbled by starving mice. More, someone to care if she never ever had sex again. Like ever.

She imagined the headlines.

Doctor's body found after three weeks! Nobody noticed recluse Poppy Spencer had died until the smell...

Or...

Miracle of regrown hymen! Autopsy of sad, lonely cat lady Poppy Spencer discovers born-again virgin...

No doubt somebody somewhere who bothered enough to listen would say she had lots of things to be thankful for. A good job—albeit varicose-vein inducing, with long hours of standing. Friends—albeit all absent. A flat—albeit leaky.

And a new, less-than-desirable flatmate, with fur. Which she would tackle, on her own, because she was a modern evolved woman...and not because she was the only person around to do it. Seriously. It was fine.

She took another decent mouthful of wine. Mr Mouse could wait; first, she'd cheer herself up and decorate the tree. Putting a hand into the box, she pulled out a bright red and silver bauble and almost cried. This was the first house-warming present Tori had bought her. Tori always bought the best presents; she had an innate sense of style.

And Poppy missed her.

'No.' More wine fortified her and put a fuzzy barrier between her and her wavering emotions. 'It's okay. I'm a grown up. I can be alone.'

She'd read, in an old tattered magazine in the doctors'

on-call room, about a famous reclusive actress who'd said that once. German? Swedish? Poppy couldn't remember; in fact things seemed to have gone a little hazy altogether.

She picked up two baubles and hung them from her ears like large, gaudy earrings, grabbed a long piece of gold tinsel and draped it round her shoulders, like an expensive wrap over her brushed-cotton, pink-checked pyjamas. Lifted her chin and spoke loudly to the street below. '*I* want to be alone. Or is it, I want to be *alone*…?'

Louder, just so she could feel the words and believe them, she shouted to the smattering of falling snowflakes illuminated by the streetlights, to the dark, cloudy sky, and to the people coming out of the Chinese takeaway with what looked like enough delicious food for a party. A far cry from her microwaved meal for one. 'It's fine. Really. You just go and enjoy yourselves with your jolly Christmas laughing and your cute bobbly hats and fifty spring rolls to share with your lovely friends and don't worry about me. I'll just stay here, on my own, and think about adopting a few stray cats or crocheting toilet-roll-holder dolls to pass the time. Crochet is the new black. It'll be good for my…fine motor skills. I'm fine. I want to *be* alone. I do.'

'Oh,' came a voice from behind her. 'In that case, I'll leave you to it. Goodnight.'

'Ah! What the hell?'

Isaac. She'd know that voice anywhere. Half posh, half street. All annoying. And very typical. Strange kind of skill he had, always turning up at her most embarrassing moments.

She winced, slowly swivelling, bringing her arms down to her sides—had she ranted out loud about her pathetic misery and lonesomeness?

Damn right she had.

The tinsel hung pathetically from her shoulders and the baubles bashed the sides of her reddening neck in a not-quite-in-tempo accompaniment to her heart rate. She probably looked a complete fool, but then, where Isaac was concerned, she was used to looking like a prize idiot.

He, however, looked his usual scruffy 'male model meets bad-boy done good' self. He needed a shave and a decent haircut; his usually cropped crew cut stood up in little tufts making him look angelic—which he wasn't. His cheeks were all pinked-up by the cold winter air. A light dusting of snow graced his shoulders. No doubt some unknowing bimbo would think he looked adorable. But Poppy knew better. Isaac's looks were deceiving.

He'd been part of the Spencer family's life for so long he was almost a member of it, and had a habit of turning up like a bad penny at the entirely wrong time, giving her that disappointed shake of his head he'd perfected over the years. But it didn't affect her quite as much as he hoped because her parents had been doing the exact same thing since she was in nappies.

And now he was here, occasionally living in her lovely flat, because her big brother, Alex, had let him rent a room without asking her first.

Isaac's head shook. Disappointedly.

She feigned nonchalance because any kind of in-depth conversation with him was the last thing on her Christmas wish-list. 'So, the missing flatmate returns.'

'I wasn't missing. I was working in Paris and then on to Amsterdam, checking out some decent bar venues.'

'Oh, lucky for some. The other day I managed to get all the way to Paddington for a sexual-health meeting, and once I even made it to the dizzy heights of Edgware Road.' She loved her job, she really did, but sometimes delving into women's unmentionables lacked any kind of glamour. And definitely no travel—apart from visiting the dark underworld of repairing episiotomies and doing cervical smears. Where she discovered a lot of women were having a lot of sex. Sadly, she wasn't one of them.

He shrugged. 'Oh. You got a whole mile away. Whoop-de-doo. Aren't you adventurous?' The animosity was a two-way thing.

He dumped his large duffel bag on the floor and threw his coat on top, cool blue eyes roving her face, then her ears, the tinsel, her flannelette pyjamas. Which had to be the most sexless items of clothing she owned. Which didn't matter. Isaac was just a flatmate. Her big brother's best friend. Nothing else.

Apart from...weird, his eyes were vivid and bright and amused. And somebody else might well have thought they were attractive, but she didn't. Not a bit. Not at all. They were too blue. Too cool. Too...*knowing*. He gave her one of his trademark long, slow smiles. Which didn't work the way he might have hoped. She did a mental body scan to check. Nope. No reaction at all.

Through her pre-pubescent years she'd done everything to garner his attention—and had probably appeared as an exasperating little diva. Then she'd woken up to the reality that he was not interested, and then neither was she once she'd discovered bigger and—she'd thought—better men to chase. Real men, not teenage boys...and then... The shame shimmied through her and burned bright in her cheeks. Eight years and she still felt it.

Well, and then Isaac had been lost in the whole sordid slipstream.

He took a step forward and plucked the tinsel from her arm between his finger and thumb, gave it a sorry little look then let it drop to the floor like an undesirable. 'I'm very sorry to have to break this to you, Poppy, but I think your Christmas fairy days might be over.'

Grabbing a bauble from her ear, she wrapped it round one of the needleless branches. Then did the same with the other one. In a last act of defiance she placed the tinsel from the floor in pride of place in the middle of the tree. 'Well, gee, thanks.'

'I just think it might be a little unstable.' He glanced up at the wonky, droopy top of the tree, then watched her sway. 'Like you perhaps?'

'Hey, be rude about me all you like, that's normal service. But you do not insult my tree.' She eyed the wine bottle behind him. No harm in a little more. 'Me and this tree have been together a long time, and no one's going to criti...be rude about it. Pass me that glass?' She pointed to the bottle and the glass and then realised that, irritating or not, she should at least be polite to him. Who knew? He might be an expert at rodent removal.

'D'you want to get yourself a glass, too? There's plenty...oh.' There appeared to be a lot of bottle and not a lot of anything in it. 'You want the last dribble? Or we could open another one?' Two bottles downed already? Now she was all out. 'Beer? Eggnog?'

'No. Thanks. I've just been working down at Blue and I've had my share for tonight.' His too-bright, too-blue eyes narrowed as his gaze roved her face again. 'And you look a little like you might have, too?'

'Hmm. I thought there was more in there. I'm just...' His smile made him look like some major celeb. She'd never noticed that before either. Gangly teenager Isaac was now pretty damned handsome? Who knew? And now he was swaying, too. *Oops*...no, it was her... What was she doing? The tree...yes, the tree. 'I just need to finish this decorating. Then I really should go to bed.'

'You need a hand?'

'Going to bed? No. I don't think—' She looked down at his palm. It was a nice hand. Slender fingers, neat nails and the slightly roughened skin of a man who worked with his hands...

Oh, and his brain. Because he was also too clever and too successful—seemed the man just knew instinctively about bars and where to put them and who to market them to. Clever, and her brother's friend. And then he'd found out her deepest, darkest secret…

Stupid. Stupid.

'No. Thanks. I'm just finishing this. You can go.' She wafted her hand to him to leave, *needed* him to leave as that memory rose, scoring the insides of her gut like sandpaper.

She slid her fist back into the decorations box. Something warm banged against it, then darted out of the hole. Something brown. Small. With more legs than she had time to count.

'Yikes!' Jumping back, she stepped on Isaac's booted foot, banged against his body—which was a whole lot firmer than she ever remembered—and ricocheted off him into an armchair, which she scrambled on, all the better to get out of the way of a man-eating furball. Her heart pounded against her ribcage. 'What…the…hell was that?'

Isaac laughed as he ducked down to the floor. 'Shh…it's just a little mouse. Very frightened now, too, by your crazy demonic scream.' He crawled along the carpet, hemming the creature into a corner, then swooped in and grabbed.

It darted away, under the TV cupboard and into a very dark corner. Now the only view Poppy had was of a very firm-looking jeans-clad backside. And a slice of skin between his belt and T-shirt, skin that for an odd reason made her tummy do a little somersault. Seemed Isaac had recently been somewhere sun-kissed as well as wintry northern Europe. 'Have you got it?'

A muffled voice came from underneath the cupboard. 'For an educated woman who uses scalpels for a living you're mighty squeamish when it comes to tiny pests. I think it's escaped.'

'You think? You *think*? I can't live here *thinking* I don't have mice. I want to *know* I don't have mice. I don't like them, they scare me, however irrational that makes me. And where there's one, there's always more. There could be fifty of them.'

'Then at least you won't be alone, right?'

'I'm fine.'

'Sure you are.' He scrambled up, looked at her all hunched up on the chair and grinned. 'So you were yelling at some poor, unsuspecting, innocent bystanders. Very loudly.'

'They were down there across the road and I'm up here behind a window. They didn't hear.'

'No. But I imagine the rest of the building did. Where is everyone?'

She slumped down, choosing not to have any more wine, because, seriously, two bottles were way more than she usually had. The mouse had done a runner, so she shovelled her feet under her backside in case it decided to retrace its teeny steps. 'They're all out. Gone. Holidays, shopping…all insanely happy and…' *Left behind.*

He perched on the arm of the chair, arms folded over his chest—looking as if he was trying to appear sympathetic but inwardly laughing. The way his face lit up when he laughed…that mouth, so nice, so weird. And maybe it was Shiraz-coloured glasses because he was so *good-looking* weird. Attractive weird. *Sexy* weird. Infuriating Isaac was eye candy, too. Who knew?

She'd been so busy being annoyed at him living in her space that she hadn't thought anything else about him at all. Apart from being aware of an electric current every time she was in the same room as him. She'd always assumed that had been caused by her anger at his general class-A irritatingness. 'Fancy them going off and having a nice time without you. Poor Poppy. Lonely?'

And he was a mind-reader, too, but no way would she fess up to such an idea. 'Don't be silly. It's great that they're all sorted—it gets them off my hands. Finally.'

'You love it, though, playing the mum, looking after them all, nurturing them…putting up the tree as a surprise for when they get home. Sweet. You don't want to be alone at all, do you?'

'You make it sound pathetic when really I'm just using you all to pay the mortgage.'

He leant towards her. 'Hey, I was joking—at least you were the sensible sibling and put your money into bricks and mortar instead of partying it away like Alex. And it's a great flat even if it does get a little busy. And leaky. But the company helps, right?'

'*Some* of the company does…'

'Don't worry, message received loud and clear. I'm sorry Alex gave me the room without talking to you first. I wouldn't have moved straight in if I'd known. But I'll be out of your hair as soon as my apartment's done.' Isaac's grin smoothed into that soft smile again and for some strange reason her unmentionables suddenly got hot and bothered.

What? No. It was just unseasonably warm tonight. Or a vasoconstrictive response to the wine. Or something. Whatever was making her body parts flush it was definitely not Isaac Blair. 'Oh, yes, the swanky South Ken penthouse. I've heard it's going to be very nice. Very swish and expensive.' Very uncluttered, too, no doubt. Isaac liked to keep things simple—most notably his love life, which, she'd observed over the years, was more like a revolving door of heartbroken women trying to ensnare him, and nothing stable or serious. Or committed. Ever. 'And the renovations will be finished when?' Hope rose.

'A couple more months, I imagine. There's Christmas

coming and everything shuts down so there'll be no progress made for a few weeks. Mid-February?'

Hope fell, but, God knew, she needed the cash to fund
her home loan. Alex might well have spent all his inheritance but he'd had a good time in the process. All she'd
got out of ploughing her grandmother's inheritance cash
into a bijou flat was a financial noose around her neck,
dodgy plumbing and four-legged furry friends. Regardless, she didn't feel overly comfortable being on her own
with Isaac and flushing unmentionables. 'Okay, so you
stay on longer than February the twenty-eighth and I'll
charge you double rent.'

His eyes widened. 'You drive a very hard bargain, Dr
Spencer.'

'Indeed I do.' Her eyes locked with his and there was
a strange rippling in the atmosphere between them. Was
she imagining it or did he feel it, too?

He dragged his gaze away, but not before she caught a
glimpse of tease there. Maybe a little heat. Whoa. Isaac?
Heat? With her? Maybe she hadn't imagined it.

'So it's just you and me here tonight, then?' he asked.

'It appears so.' And why did that make her feel suddenly nervous? No, not nervous...tingly. Tingly happened
to other people. Not her.

She looked across the wooden floor to the dark hole
under the TV and tingly mingled with fear. Although she
had to admit she did feel a lot better with Isaac in the flat.
'Just you, me and our furry friend, of course...plus his
babies, wife, mother, grandparents, probably a community
the size of a small tropical nation living in the rafters, the
walls...under my bed.'

'I'll get a trap tomorrow from the hardware stall at the
market and have a word with the café and let them know
we have guests. They'll need to know for their own health
and safety measures.'

'Oh, I don't want it hurt, or dead. I just want it gone. Out of here.'

'Like me? Right.'

Got it in one. She couldn't hide the smile. 'You can stay if you can keep the rodent population to a minimum. Humanely. Yes. Yes. The mice. Do things…with them.' Was she rambling a little?

'Is that all I'm good for, really?'

She could think of a few things—starting with that mouth. Her stomach joined her head in all kinds of woozy. Definitely too much alcohol on an empty stomach. 'I'm sure you're good for a lot of things, Isaac…'

'I've never had any complaints.' He stood up, the flash of cheekiness gone. She wondered how it would be to really flirt with him, just a little. But then she didn't know how. He brushed down his T-shirt and strode towards his bag.

There was something she was supposed to ask him. She couldn't remember… Something about work or Christmas… Her head was getting foggy… Oh, yes… She held up a finger. 'Wait. One thing.'

He stopped and turned, the bag still in his hand. 'Yes?'

'I have a problem.'

Smug eyebrows peaked. 'Oh? Just the one?'

'Don't be cheeky. I'm organising the department Christmas party and the venue has double-booked us. Any chance Blue could fit us in? I'm in a bit of a pickle because I'm organising the party…' Had she already said that? He might just save the day. She put her hand on one hip and flashed him her best winning smile. 'Pretty please?'

It appeared to have little effect apart from the eyebrows rising further. 'Now you're just being nice because you want something. Poppy, Poppy, should I charge you double rates, too? What night?'

'Next Friday.'

'I'll check the diary tomorrow. Shouldn't be a problem, though. That's early for a Christmas party.'

'Things tend to hot up the closer we get to Christmas. Everyone wants a Christmas baby so they either try to hold on…or try to get it out early. We want to get the party out of the way so we can focus.' Focusing was a bit of a problem right now, but she figured she'd be fine by Christmas.

'So you're working over Christmas? Not going home?'

She snorted at the thought. 'You're joking, right? I offered to work Christmas Day so the staff with families that actually cared for each other could spend time together. That way I have a good excuse to stay away from the family pile. So do me a favour and make sure my work Christmas party's a good one? I want at least one thing to look forward to this festive season.' *Give me a good time, Isaac?*

Geez, she was funny.

'Okay, I'll see what I can do. And now, I'm definitely going to bed.' He turned again, his back straight, shoulders solid and that backside giftwrapped in jeans, all tight and firm and…her mouth watered.

What in hell was she thinking?

She watched him reach the door and felt an overwhelming desire to talk to him just a little more. She didn't want to be on her own. And for some reason she felt a tingling down low and a need to…to what?

She hadn't been able to think about sex for so long and now…well, right now she was thinking about it a lot. And not just because she was on the obstetrics and gynaecology rotation, although if that job taught her anything it was that women were either doing it a lot or not able to do it and wanting her to fix problems so they could do it some more.

But she deserved a little fun—and some much needed sexperience—maybe Isaac would know how she could find some. 'Hey, Isaac, wait.'

'What now?'

'You have fun, right?'

She couldn't read his expression as he turned to face her. Something between grumpy and irritated. And downright insanely sexy. 'Sure. I work hard so I figure I should play hard, too.'

'That's it...that's just it, right there. I've worked so hard for so long and I just want...*more*. Is there more? What more is there? What am I missing? How do you... you know, have fun without getting messed up in the process? Do you understand?' She wasn't sure she did. Not a lot of anything made sense right now. Except that Isaac had come closer and was looking at her with those bluest of blue eyes—okay, he was a little out of focus... And she wanted to stroke his hair. No, she wanted to breathe in his smell. It was smoky, very masculine. Yummy. She wanted to breathe him in and stroke his hair. 'Is there more, Isaac?'

'Oh. Okay, I see, we're at stage three already.' He disappeared into the kitchen and brought back a pint glass filled with water. 'Drink this.'

She took a sip. He pushed it back towards her mouth and she drank a whole lot more; it was refreshing but nowhere near as nice as the Shiraz. 'Stage three of what?'

'It goes like this. The tipsy stage. The funny stage. The "pondering the universe" stage. Then, the "I love you, you're my bestest ever friend" stage. And finally, the up-chuck. We see it all the time at work and, trust me, you do not want to get to stage five.'

She put the glass down on the coffee table. 'I am so not at any stage.'

'Walk in a straight line, then, preferably towards your bedroom to sleep the alcohol off.'

She doubted she could stand in a straight line. 'I don't have to. I'm fine, thank you very much. Very fine indeedy.'

He held her gaze. A challenge. The heat in his eyes was flecked with serious. So nice. So very, very nice.

And very, very Isaac. 'Okay, okay, I'll walk.' Oh, yes, she could do that. She could do that perfectly; show Isaac Blair she wasn't afraid of any challenge from him.

CHAPTER TWO

STAGE THREE. WITHOUT a doubt things could well get messy. After spending hours dealing with this kind of stuff at work Isaac really did not need it at home, too, but he took Poppy's hand and pulled her up from the chair. For the second time that night she bumped against him and he steadied her, feeling the softness of her body as she leaned into him. Cute that she wore old-fashioned pyjamas to bed, but with Poppy's slightly restrained approach to life it wasn't surprising.

The way she felt was, though. She had curves where curves should very definitely be and right now, pressed against him, they certainly chased away the London winter chill.

Hell, she'd grown up. A lot. And even though he'd caught up with her over the years he hadn't really looked at her. Hadn't wanted to—and she clearly hadn't wanted anything to do with him either. Not since the night he'd held her thick dark hair while she vomited into a rose bush and cried for a man who wasn't him. 'Hey, careful.'

'Oops. Sorry.' She looked up at him through a fringe that grazed long black eyelashes and something flashed behind her deep brown eyes. Caution. Poppy's normal mojo. She'd trodden a safe, sensible path for the last however many years—never letting herself get out of control, always steadily working towards her career goal. But there was something else in those eyes, too—something glittering—need? Lust?

First time he'd seen her let her guard down in for ever. Amazing what a bit of wine could do.

'Right.' He stretched a piece of tinsel along the floor. Hell, it wasn't his problem; *she* wasn't his problem. But he had to make sure she was safe. Way he saw it, he could probably do this tinsel line straight to her bedroom and she'd hardly notice. 'Now, walk along this line and we'll see what stage you're at. Then you should definitely get some shut-eye.'

'See. I can do this, *no problemo.*' Her right foot rested on top of the tinsel, scarlet-painted toes pointed as if she were perfecting a gymnastic display on the barre. Left foot. Then the right flailed in mid-air, she wobbled, fell sideways and into his outstretched arms. She grabbed on to his shoulder and he got a whiff of clean citrus, shampoo possibly or shower gel. The woman smelt good. She smiled. 'Oops again. You're a good catcher, Isaac. Thank you for being here. You're very kind. Very nice actually, I think. Underneath that standoffish mask. Very nice indeed. We could be friends, you know… You know a lot about me. More than anyone—'

'Shh. Let's concentrate on the walking thing.' He placed a finger over her lips. Rapidly approaching stage four—he did not want to deal with that. 'Then I think we should get you to bed.'

'Absolutely… Is that…is that an offer?' The heat in her body slammed against his. Her lips parted ever so slightly as she smiled.

Then closed again as he shook his head. 'Thanks. But, no. If we were ever to do anything in bed, Poppy…which we won't…I'd want you to be able to remember it in the morning.'

Sleeping with Poppy? Insane idea. But the thought lingered for just too long, and he hadn't been with a woman in a while.

Absolutely not.

He gently removed her from his arm, and within a nanosecond of that touch his body zinged with a shot of pure feral desire. Here she was offering herself to him, this attractive grown-up woman—although he'd only just awoken to that fact. He could take her to bed and ease away some of the stresses of the past week. Show her the fun she so obviously craved.

Only, this was Poppy and there were a dozen or more reasons why that would be the worst damned idea he'd had in a long time. Not least the fact she was drunk, lonely and, until she'd uttered that last sentence, he would have sworn she hated his guts. He'd been there at her lowest, her weakest and worst moment, and somehow she'd never forgiven him.

Not that he'd ever cared. Impressing women past a flirty dalliance had never been on his agenda. He'd spent enough time watching too many marriages fail to contemplate one himself, and he wasn't about to change that any time soon.

It had been a busy few days—he was tired, was all, having put every ounce of effort into getting the Paris bar up and running. He needed sleep. On his own. 'Come on, let's get you to the bedroom.'

'No! Bathroom first. Teeth. Floss. Wee.'

'Too much information, lady.' For some reason his hand seemed to have slipped back round her waist. She wasn't so drunk that she'd fall over, but he thought it best he should steady her as they walked towards the bathroom. Her head rested against his shoulder and she looked sweet. Smelt great. Felt…sexy as all hell. Was it possible to be jet-lagged from a one-hour flight? Because he couldn't think of any other reason for this strange disorientation.

He tried to keep his eyes on the bathroom decor and

not on Poppy's backside as she dipped to rinse her tooth-brush. She'd done a reasonable job painting the flat in bright, light colours. The bathroom still needed a little TLC as the plumbing was cranky at best but it was clean and tiled in muted stone. A large skylight shed light from above although now all he could see were glimpses of stars in a cloudy night sky.

What gave the room colour were the multi-hued bits of lace drying on the radiator on the far wall. Still unused to sharing a house with so many women, he wondered what the correct response should be to finding flimsy under-wear wherever he looked. He doubted it should be the spike of interest, and trying to match the panties to the woman. Now he tried not to imagine Poppy in the red and black number.

Hey, he was a hot-blooded man after all.

After a few moments of brushing her teeth she looked at him through the reflection in the large mirror. 'You know it's a medical impossibility to become a virgin again once you're not. Right?'

'Uh-huh. You're the doctor, not me. But I think it's a given that once the seal is broken it can't exactly be unbro-ken. And where are you going with this, Miss Einstein?' Grabbing the towel, she dried her mouth, then turned to him.

'I'm a fraud. I advise women every day about their sex lives and I don't have one. How can I talk to them about sex when I don't even remember what it's like? I don't want to be an almost-virgin when I die, Isaac, but I'm headed that way.'

Like he was the right guy to be having this conversa-tion with. Especially when he was the only person in the universe who knew why she'd given up sex. Anger started to rise from nowhere. She'd run away from any kind of relationship ever since, when she could have been happy.

Happier. 'You really do need to sleep off that wine. There's plenty of time to get a sex life and plenty of men who, I'm sure, would be willing to help you in your…dilemma.'

'Would you?' Those pretty painted toes took a step towards him.

'Would I what?'

But instead of answering in words, she pressed her mouth against his. Pressed her body against his. Made little mewling sounds that activated every hot-blooded cell in his body. And, hell, he should have pulled away, put her straight to bed and left. But she tasted so damned good…

Someone was playing bongo drums in Poppy's head. And someone else was stomping in her stomach. Her throat hurt. Her mouth was dry. She felt like hell.

Worse than hell.

After a couple of minutes stabilising herself she twisted in the sheets about to sit up but her foot collided against something warm. Something large. In her bed. Her eyelids shot open and she managed to stifle the scream in her throat, holding her breath as she tried to make sense of it. Her heart thumped in conjunction with the annoying beat in her head as her toes gingerly tested the object.

A leg. Human. Hairy.

What. The. Hell?

She closed her eyes again until her stomach stopped churning. There was a man in her bed.

Isaac?

It took all of her strength to turn over quietly so as not to waken him up. Yes—same hair, same smell. She clamped her eyes closed again.

Isaac.

A bare leg. Two bare legs. She felt down her front…no cosy pink flannelette pyjamas, but a skimpy silk cami top? No PJ bottoms, but matching silk and lace French knickers? Lara's expensive design—for best times only. What in hell had she done?

Please no.

Surely not?

Surely, surely not? She'd spent the night with a man. With Isaac. First time in eight long years and she couldn't even remember it?

The vodka and Coke she'd had at the pub before she came home she easily remembered. And…ugh…the red wine gifts from her clients. Bile rose to her throat. She was never ever drinking again. Fuzzy flickering images of Isaac arriving while she was putting up the tree gradually came into focus. But how had they gone from that, to…this?

But oh, oh, God…she suddenly remembered kissing him in the bathroom. Remembered how she'd felt bold and brave and very sexy. And how he'd tasted so nice, his kiss so tender… Even now she could smell his scent, firing flashes of heat through her belly.

'Sleeping Beauty finally wakes up.' He turned, naked shoulders peeking out from her sheets, sat up, eyes as bright as the daylight splicing through her curtains. His hair was mussed up and he looked devastatingly hot. 'Sleep well? Eventually?'

'Why are you in my bed?' Bunching the sheet around her throat, she sat up, too. No way was she getting out until he'd gone.

'You don't remember, Poppy? What a shame. It was a spectacular night and you don't remember at all? I'm so disappointed.'

There was that shake of the head she knew so well. Daddy Spencer would be a proud man to see someone perfect that frown, even if it wasn't his own flesh and blood.

'I remember…we kissed.' *Oh, God, kill me now.* 'And

then…' She tried to force the cogs in her brain to work harder, faster, but they were stuck in fog. 'Not a lot else.'

His hands clasped at the back of his neck showing mighty fine pectoral muscles, impressive biceps… Her mouth dried to something beyond the Sahara. Mortified she might have been, but she could still take time out to appreciate a beautiful human specimen when she saw one. She'd touched that? Lain under that? Or had she been on top? Or both? Who knew?

Aargh! Why couldn't she remember?

He appeared to be struggling to keep a straight face. 'You surprised even me. And I'm used to pretty much anything. Not exactly a screamer, more a gasper…'

'A gasper? I didn't… We didn't…?' A flash of him running his hand through her hair emerged through the soup in her brain. No, that had been years ago. But…the image in her head was of her current bathroom. Of safe hands stroking her back. A soft smile as he'd picked her up and carried her across the apartment and into her bedroom.

'You kissed me.' No way would she forget that in a London minute.

'No, Poppy. You kissed me.'

'You kissed me back.'

Those magnificent shoulders shrugged. 'Glad to help out a lady in need. You said you wanted me to teach you a few things. Asked me…begged me.'

Oh, good Lord. Begged Isaac? 'Well, that was the vodka talking.'

'Vodka? No, a couple of bottles of Aussie Shiraz by the looks of it.'

Her stomach lurched with just the thought of it. She swallowed hard. 'Vodka with colleagues in the pub before the wine on my own.' Could it get any worse? He'd kissed her because she'd asked him to help her. Begged him. Not because he'd fancied her. Not because he'd wanted her. He'd kissed her out of pity.

She'd begged him?

'I have to say you are an almost textbook drunk.'

'Good to know.' That'd be right. Usually Poppy did everything by the book, because not doing so caused too much harm and mayhem. And she never wanted to go there again.

'But what is it about me, Popsicle?' His use of her childhood nickname made her cringe, and he damn well knew it, making her pull the sheets more tightly round her cleavage as he spoke. 'Is it something I do? Is it the way I smell? Every time we get a moment alone we end up with your head down, bum up. Gasping. Stage five implemented to perfection. You are a champion upchucker.'

No. Not again. 'I was sick?'

'Yes. Spectacularly.'

'I'm so sorry.' No wonder her stomach hurt.

'Not pretty.'

'So we didn't, er, you know.'

He shrugged. 'Hey, you know me, I never give away our secrets.'

She'd begged him not to before and he'd been true to his word. She threw him a glance—his grin widened and she wasn't sure if he was referring to back then or last night. But he was clearly not going to enlighten her. Irritating.

Over the ensuing years that evening had hovered between them like an ominous dark cloud—would he ever confront her? Would he put her in a situation where she'd have to confess to everyone what she'd done and show who the real Poppy Spencer was?

So far he'd kept schtum on the whole thing—but then she'd never allowed herself to be in any kind of situation where she owed him anything more. And ever since then the all-new shiny reformed Poppy Spencer hadn't put a foot wrong.

But still—he *knew*. And for that reason alone she kept him at a distance.

Fast forward to the second most mortifying moment of her life—if they'd actually done the deed surely she'd know? She'd feel different—her body would feel less nauseated and more...excited. Surely? No, they hadn't had sex, she was pretty certain. Relief flooded through her. 'So why are you in my bed now? Why am I in different clothes? Where are my pyjamas?'

His head shook. Disappointedly. 'Don't panic, I put a quick stop to the kiss and you're still an *almost*-virgin.'

'A what?'

'Never mind. Just something you said last night. Amongst a whole lot of other stuff.' His voice rose a couple of octaves. ' *"Please don't leave me, there's a mouse on the run. I'm scared. Too cold. Too hot. I need a drink. Headache. I'm going to be sick again. Please, don't leave me, Isaac, I'm scared."* Eventually your demands exhausted me and I fell asleep right here. You are one hell of a snorer, by the way. I hope for your sake it was just because of the alcohol.' He smiled his slow, lazy smile. 'And now you're wearing the only things I could lay my hands on in the dark at four-thirty this morning during the too-hot phase. Very, very nice, too.'

His eyebrows rose as his fingers plucked the blush-pink lacy straps of her cami. At his touch her body reacted in a very un-Poppy-like way—with a frenzied surge of what she could only describe as lust. And he knew it, too, judging by the glittering in his eyes. 'Must have cost a fair bit.'

She slapped his hand away from her straps, not least because of the effect his skin was having on her skin. 'They did, even with mate's rates. And did you look...did you see...?' She'd learnt to be forthright with her patients;

why couldn't she be forthright with him? She needed to know the extent of her absolute mortification. She took a deep breath, not wanting to hear the answer to her question. 'Okay, so who undressed me? Did you help with that or did I manage it all by myself?'

'Don't worry, I closed my eyes.' He leaned forward and whispered against her neck, making her shiver and shudder and hot and cold at the same time. 'Most of the time.'

'What? No!'

Then he winked. 'All I can say is that someone's going to be a very lucky man one day.' But he clearly wasn't referring to himself because with that he threw the sheet back, revealing a pair of extremely well-toned legs, thigh-hugging black boxers with the outlined shape of something she only allowed herself a moment's glance at before she was totally and utterly lost for words... Wow...just wow. And a body that she could have sworn she saw advertising aftershave in a glossy yesterday. 'Got to get to work, Popsicle. I'll make sure I get a mousetrap on the way back. Thanks for a very entertaining evening.'

Then he was gone.

'Damn. Damn. Damn.' She leaned back against the pillows and breathed out a huge sigh, unsure of what to make of it all. Because, despite the Macarena in her stomach, she could have sworn she should be feeling a whole lot different from the way she felt right now. She should definitely not be feeling turned on. Her breasts should not be tingly, her heart should not be pounding, her lady bits should definitely not be wide awake and singing hallelujah at the mere hint of Isaac's presence. Or at the thought of him seeing her naked. No. She should not be feeling like this at all. Especially when the startling, belittling, humiliating truth of it all was that, without any thought of consequences, she'd got drunk, accosted him and he'd kissed her back *out of pity*.

CHAPTER THREE

'WE HAVE MICE. At least, we've seen one little critter upstairs. I thought I should let you know.' Isaac paid for his coffee and nodded his thanks to Marco, the café owner. 'I've got a couple of traps and we'll sort it out our end. Just keep an eye out down here in case they migrate.'

'Okay, cheers, mate, I'll have a look, but we're usually on top of zeez things. No mices here.' Marco pushed Isaac's coffee towards him and started to serve the next customer.

Isaac took his cup, negotiated the defunct fireman's pole that connected their upstairs apartment with Ignite café, and found a seat, aiming to fortify his strength with a sharp caffeine buzz before he nipped back to the flat. The last thing he wanted was to bump into Poppy and relive the awkwardness of earlier. A coffee shot would help. Plus keep him awake for the long night's work ahead.

He took a sip. Added an extra sugar for luck. Opened his smartphone and reviewed his notes. The only thing of any consequence he'd managed to achieve today was to check the availability of the bar for Friday, for Poppy. Then he'd sorted out a mousetrap, for Poppy. Spoken to the manager at Ignite café, for Poppy. And hidden in the café, *from* Poppy. The woman was invading his every living, breathing moment, not to mention his to-do list.

Which was very interesting. He never allowed any

woman to ever invade anything at all. Work came first. Always. Work was predictable and straightforward. Work didn't change the goalposts or come with an agenda that you didn't understand. He knew where he stood with his business—knew what he needed to do to be the best. And he'd made damned sure he had been, throwing hour after hour, year after year into transforming his bars into award-winning establishments. Being pretty much uprooted and homeless by the age of sixteen, he was used to travelling, liked the challenge of working in different countries, of winning the hearts and loyalty of the Parisians and the Dutch. Next stop, the States, and he'd be a success there, too. That would show everyone who'd ever doubted him.

But despite what he'd said and what he'd tried to convince himself to believe, he'd really enjoyed that kiss. The cheeky glimpse of Poppy's half-naked body bathed in moonlight hadn't been half bad either. Which, hands on heart, had not been his fault. She'd said she was ready, when in reality her silky top hadn't quite covered everything it needed to. He'd turned away…too late.

Hell. He closed his eyes briefly at the mental image; she was definitely all woman. And off every limit he had. So the fact his brain kept wandering back to those scenes last night—the kiss, her body, her smell, even her pyjamas—was very inconvenient.

He added *fast-track the renovations* to his to-do list. He could control his libido, but he couldn't guarantee for how long, so the sooner he was out of that flat, the better. Stupid enough to get in any way involved with a woman, doubly so to get carried away with a woman he had too much history with. That could get all kinds of messy.

Isaac subscribed to the 'no promises, no commitment, no heartbreak' school of relationships. Easy. In his bitter experience commitment usually lasted just until someone *better, richer, younger* came along, leaving chaos and hurt in the slipstream. He didn't need any of that.

The doorbell pinged behind him as someone entered along with the cold December wind-chill factor. Women's voices. His gut pinged, too, as his hand froze, coffee cup halfway between the table and his mouth. Izzy's northern-infused accent. Poppy's hesitant laughter.

So much for avoiding her.

Gulping the too-hot coffee and almost suffering third-degree burns in the process, he put his cup on the table, tugged up his coat collar around his ears, focused on his phone and concentrated on trying to be incognito. Plan A: when they started to order at the counter he'd slip out unnoticed.

'Isaac! Hello.' Izzy dropped a kiss on his cheek, then shoved a stray lock of short blond hair behind her ear, beaming. He'd met a lot of Poppy's friends over the years, as part of a peripheral group that tagged along whenever Poppy's brother, Alex, was home on leave, but never had he envisaged living with any of them. Strange how life worked out. 'Long time no see. Where've you been?'

'Hi, Izzy. Hello, Poppy. I was in Europe for a while sussing out some bar venues. We've just opened one in Bastille and we've another planned for Amsterdam.' He tried to focus on Izzy, but his eyes kept drifting towards the woman he'd spent the night with. She refused to meet his gaze, keeping her focus on the counter ahead, then on Izzy, a small polite wave to Marco. Scraping his chair back, Isaac lifted his plastic carrier. 'I got some traps. I'll head upstairs now and set them up. Do you have any peanut butter?'

Finally Poppy looked up at him, her make-up-free cheeks pinking. Instead of her regulation work ponytail her hair hung in loose curls around her shoulders, which normally would have made her look younger, if it hadn't been for the purple shadows under her eyes.

She pulled a thick cream cardigan around her uptight shoulders and stamped black suede boots on the tiles. Her mouth had formed a grim line. Clearly the hangover still hung.

Even so, she still looked breathtaking. He'd never really thought of her like that until yesterday. But breathtaking was the only way to describe her. Yeah…well, she'd certainly taken his breath away with that surprise kiss last night. As she spoke he wondered what could happen next time, if he left his principles at the bedroom door. Which was never going to happen. Because he would never let them get into that situation again.

She frowned. 'I thought mice ate cheese.'

'The guy in the market said to use peanut butter— apparently they love it. If we don't have any I'll head to the shop and get some.'

'No. There's some in the cupboard by the fridge.' She peered up at him. 'Smooth.'

'Thanks. I like to think so.' He grinned.

'Yeah, Mr Big Shot, whatever. I was talking about the peanut butter, not you.' She tutted, her shoulders dropping a little as her eyebrows rose. 'You definitely fall in the crunchy camp.'

'Oh, and now I'm mortally wounded.' Still, it was good to have her at least being able to look at him. Things could get weird in the flat if they couldn't speak to each other. 'Well, I've got to set these traps then get back to work… Oh, talking of…the private room's free at Blue on Friday for your work get-together if you still want it. Do you need to come and view it?'

'No, I don't think—' She looked off-balance and not particularly thrilled at having this conversation.

'Or are you fine taking my word for it?' He could give

them both a get-out if he sorted it all here. Then he could head off to his sanctuary and work out what the hell was going on in his head. Or at the very least try and get her out of it. 'How many will be coming? Do you need food? I can get the chef to make up a specials menu for you all.'

'I think there's probably about twenty of us, including some spouses and partners.' She matched his smile. Not too friendly. 'I'm sure the regular menu will be fine.'

Good, no need to spend any more time with her than necessary. 'Great. I'll see you later. Some time. I'm kind of busy at the bar so I might not be around much.'

Way to go—Poppy's whole demeanour seemed to brighten. 'Oh—okay.'

'Wait. Isaac?' Izzy interrupted and his optimism floundered. 'Maybe Poppy and I should come over this afternoon. I'd love to see your new bar. I'm scouting out places for the wedding reception. And Poppy? How can you organise a party without checking out the venue first?'

'Oh, I trust Isaac,' she said in a voice that conveyed the opposite. 'I'm sure it'll be fine.'

Izzy looked at her friend with growing incredulity. 'It's a cocktail bar, right? And you're on a day off?'

Poppy gave a weak shrug. 'Yes. Actually, just for a change I have some time off. And I was hanging out for a coffee. You know Marco makes a mean espresso.'

'Forget the coffee. What are we waiting for? Blue awaits. Come on, bride-to-be's prerogative.' Blissfully ignorant of the awkwardness in the room as she rode her fluffy happy wedding cloud, Izzy smiled. 'A cocktail will be fun. Happy hour for mates, okay, Isaac?'

Looked as if he had no choice.

Looked as if none of them had a choice. The bride-to-be certainly did hold all the cards.

Poppy shook her head as she wiggled out of Izzy's hold and held up her hands. 'No, I'm sorry, not today, we can go to Blue some other time. Come along with us on Friday if you want—there'll be quite a crowd. But as from today I'm officially on the wagon. I'm never drinking again.'

'Why ever not?' Izzy asked. 'It's Christmas time. We have to drink and be merry. It's the rule.'

'I had too much last night. You know me, I'm a very cheap date and rubbish at holding my booze.'

As Isaac well knew, to the detriment of a sane mind and a decent night's sleep. And that kiss that made his mouth water for more. 'Oh, don't worry, Poppy, I'm sure we can rustle you up a virgin margarita. Or even—' he made sure he had her full attention '—an *almost*-virgin one.'

'Why do you keep...?' Her cheeks blazed and she looked down at her boots. When she lifted her chin again realisation flamed in her eyes. 'Oh, my God. I didn't...?'

'Didn't what?' Izzy's eyebrows formed a V. She looked first at Poppy and then at Isaac. 'What are you two talking about? What didn't you do?'

Isaac saw the pain on Poppy's face and knew he'd stepped too far. She did sarcasm like a pro, but had also relied on him to hold her secrets close to his chest, and he'd never been tempted to share them so he wasn't going to start now. Although sometimes she was a little too damned serious for her own good. Honestly, she didn't need to repent for ever. Everyone had at least one thing in their past they regretted. And being sexually inexperienced wasn't exactly a crime. Some man would be very lucky indeed to reintroduce Poppy to the dating scene. Isaac only hoped it wouldn't be a jerk like the last one.

And why did the thought of Poppy with another man make his blood pressure hike? Things weren't making sense today. 'Didn't...get to sort out the rest of the tree decorations. Right, Poppy? Maybe you and Izzy could finish them this afternoon.' *And stay out of my way.*

Izzy picked up her bags and shook her head. 'Rubbish.

We'll come with you to set the traps. I'm so glad you've chosen the humane ones—I'd hate to see anything get hurt. We can be The Three Mouseketeers, releasing the mice into their true habitat outdoors. You must call me if you catch any. I'd love to see them. Then we'll tag along and see what an amazing bar you've created, Isaac. I've heard so much about it.' She turned to Poppy. 'Come on, please? I don't get the chance to do this very often. I feel like living dangerously. Okay?'

'Oh, okay. Just a quick drink, but I'm on water.' Poppy sighed.

And for just a second he was back in that bed watching as she fell asleep. How many times had he shared his bed? Too many to count. And no woman sleeping had made his heart squeeze as she had last night, as if he'd wanted to protect her, to stop her feeling as rotten as she clearly felt. To stop her needing to outright ask for a sexual experience. The accidental glimpse of a woman's nipples hadn't ever before made him feel so aroused.

No woman had looked so damned hot with a hangover either.

His groin tightened as he watched her. Goddamn—he needed a bit of distance, not to give her a guided tour of his bar.

Catching Isaac's eye, she frowned and shook her head minutely, but just enough for him to understand. He got the message loud and clear. *Don't mention it, don't think about it and definitely don't ever consider spending another night in my bed.*

Which was one hundred per cent fine by him.

Blue lived up to the hype. Even through foggy hangover vision Poppy could see why Isaac had won the Best New Bar Award this year. Decorated in vivid midnight blue with a wall of cascading turquoise water in the centre of what used to be a bank it was startling, edgy and yet a very comfortable place to be with soft, plump easy chairs she sank into.

Or would have been comfortable if she hadn't been in direct eye line of Isaac all afternoon, on tenterhooks wondering what the heck he was going to say and how she was going to answer. He'd always had slick one-liners, been far too cocky for his own good and she was so out of her league here—tongue-tied with embarrassment.

As it was mid-afternoon the place was quiet with just a couple of other customers sitting up at the long mahogany bar reading the extensive cocktail menu. Izzy tapped her martini glass against Poppy's sparkling water. 'Cheers. I'm very impressed—no wonder he's doing so well if all his bars are like this. He's a bit of a mystery, though, isn't he? Flitting in and out of the country... He's sort of been vaguely around the edge of our group on and off for years, then he's suddenly rich and successful and renting a room at yours.'

Poppy nodded. 'Believe me, the renting's only temporary. He wouldn't have been my first choice of flatmate. But when Alex offered him your old room I couldn't exactly say no. I guess Alex thought he was doing us both a favour.'

Izzy winced. 'Sorry. I didn't mean to leave you in a mess.'

'Ah, look, I'm a landlady, I have to expect these things to happen. Funny, though, we were so settled for all those years, just you, me and Tori in our lovely flat.'

'*Your* lovely flat.'

'Yes, well, I always thought of it as ours really—you helped me find it and decorate it. I just bankrolled it. But then in the space of two months everything's changed so much I can barely keep up. Tori moved out to be with Mark, and you moved out to live with Harry. Alex moved in, Tori moved back into the box room, Isaac took your old room. And just to spice things up a bit, we had Matt for a month. I'm getting a bit dizzy. It's like the place has a revolving door at the moment.' If only Isaac could see fit to revolve out permanently instead of staying over for a few nights here and there…usually unannounced. Still, paying full rent in advance meant his contribution to the mortgage was a big relief to her money worries. In the short term. 'Besides, with his job he's hardly around.' Until recently. Now it felt as if he was around rather too much for her liking.

'And he hasn't got a girlfriend? Or at least no woman to stay with until his flat's ready.'

'Oh, trust me, he's had plenty of women.' Poppy sipped her water and thought briefly about exchanging it for something stronger so she could find some of the bravado she must have had last night. Kissing someone—not even asking, just kissing—took guts. She hadn't known she had any. Not those kind of guts, anyway. Asking for what she wanted, taking what she wanted. Typical it had ended in disaster.

Izzy clarified, 'No long-term woman.'

'According to Alex, Isaac's dating record is a month. Thirty days. That's not enough to give anything a chance. I've heard of the kind of things he used to get up to with Alex and it's not pretty. The man's just a flirt. No self-respecting woman would want long term with him, anyway, not that he'd ever offer. I think watching his mother have failed marriage after failed marriage has put him off any kind of commitment.' So said the ex–junior psychiatrist in her.

She watched him so comfortable there behind the bar with his colleagues, laughing and joking. The smart shirt accentuated the pecs of steel she'd seen this morning. Her mind drifted back to the tight boxers and her heart rate escalated. She swallowed another gulp of water to douse an unexpected heat rushing through her. *God.* Hot and bothered just by looking at a man. This never happened. Never. Was she eighteen again?

Ugh. She shuddered. She damned well hoped not.

'There's a funny vibe between you two. There's always been a funny vibe, but it's getting more *vib*rant.'

Bless Izzy and her wishful happyed-up thinking. 'There's no *vibe*.'

Her friend touched her arm. 'Just be careful.'

This was the girl Poppy had known for ever. Only once had she ever kept a secret from her; every other single thing about their lives they had shared. Openly. Everything. And yet she didn't want to tell Izzy about last night, about kissing Isaac and the weird sensations he was instilling in her. Didn't want to confess about the hole she felt she had in her personal life and the inadequacies in her professional one. All of which could be fixed by one kind, considerate and caring man and a little sexperience. Isaac did not fit that bill.

But inside her head the only image was of naked shoulders peeking out of her sheets. Too-blue eyes teasing, hot breath on her neck, and tight black boxers. Always the black boxers.

Everything tingled. Every damned thing. 'Me and Isaac? I don't think so. Seriously.'

Izzy nodded. 'You're probably right—too close to home. Too weird after all these years. He's definitely good to look at though.'

'Says the married-woman-to-be.'

'Hey, I'm getting married, not joining a convent.' Izzy drained her glass. 'I said be careful, I didn't say don't act on the vibe. You could always just have a little...' her eyes widened '...fun.'

Sexual fun? She'd have to look that up in the dictionary.

A crash and the sound of breaking glass had them turning to look back to the bar. Isaac was holding a towel over one of the barmen's hands. He turned to look at her directly, raised his eyebrows summoning her over. The day was rapidly spiralling into disaster. This was not how she'd planned to spend her holiday.

She stood, wishing that she'd chosen flower arranging instead of medicine as her vocation, then she wouldn't need to be near him. Smelling him. Thinking about the black boxers. *Ahem. Medical emergency?*

She dragged on her game face. 'Looks like I'm needed. Duty calls.'

Izzy stood, too, and grabbed her bags. 'Do you want me to stay and help?'

'No. I'll be fine. You go. Aren't you supposed to be meeting Harry?'

'Yes, but…I don't want to leave you.'

'Seriously, I'm a doctor, I can manage. You go, this could take a little time. See you later.'

'Hey, thanks for coming over.' Isaac looked at the grimacing man and then back to Poppy. 'My friend Poppy, here, is a doctor, very handy to have around. Jamie's my business partner and he's just had a contretemps with a glass. Got a nasty cut—do you think it'll need stitches? I've got a first-aid kit.'

Ignoring the *thud-thud* of her heart as she got closer to the one person she should have been far away from, she pulled back the towel and peered at the gash. 'It's pretty deep. Yes. Yes, it needs sutures and I don't have anything with me. Your first-aid kit probably won't do. You'll have to go to A and E or a GP surgery, I'm afraid.'

Isaac walked the barman to the seating area out front. 'Okay, Jamie, sit down, mate. I'll call a cab and come with you.'

'And close up the bar? Don't be daft.'

Poppy shook her head, grasping the 'get out of jail free' card. 'I can go with you if you like? This is my kind of territory. I might be able to fast-track you through.'

Jamie looked at them both in turn. 'Er…seriously? I stopped needing a nanny in primary school. It's a cut hand, is all. Just get me a taxi and I'll sort the rest. It'll leave you short for tonight though, Isaac. Sorry, mate.'

'Not your problem. Just get it fixed. I'll be fine.'

'With the Christmas cocktail lesson starting in thirty minutes? You reckon? How about you call Maisie in?'

Isaac frowned. 'She's gone to Oxford with her boyfriend.'

'Carl?'

The frown deepened. 'At some uni event. No worries, I'll be fine. I can manage.'

Jamie turned to Poppy, holding his hand close to his chest. Blood seeped through the towel, vivid red contrasting with his blanching complexion. He needed to be gone and quick. 'I know this is a long shot, but I don't suppose you have any bar experience, do you?'

Spend more time with the man she'd shared a bed with? And who her body appeared to want a repeat performance with. This time, with full body contact?

No way. 'Me? No. Not really.'

Jamie's shoulders slumped. 'Just for a couple of hours until I get back, or Isaac can get reinforcements?'

She looked at them both staring at her. Jamie hopeful. Isaac not so much. But heck, she had nothing to do for the next few hours…days…and no one to do it with. She might as well stay and be of use to someone as sit at home with four-legged furry friends and a bent Christmas tree. 'I… well, I could collect glasses and take orders, I suppose.'

Isaac looked less than thrilled but relieved. 'Are you sure? Thanks. Most excellent. That would be a great help. I can teach the class, no problem, it's just the serving I need a hand with.' He pressed a chaste kiss to her cheek that sent shock waves of lust shivering through her. This was such a bad idea. 'You're a star.'

'I know.'

As they watched Jamie leave in the taxi, Isaac stepped closer, eyes twinkling. 'You never know, Popsicle, you might learn a few things. Cocktails are my speciality. Especially virgi—'

'No. Don't say it. Don't even go there.' She stabbed a finger into that hard wall of muscle he had for a chest, resisting the sudden urge to fist his shirt and pull him closer and press her lips to his again—just to remind her what he tasted like. 'I'm doing this because you looked after me last night. Because you're letting me have the private room for my party. And because you bought a mousetrap. After this we'll be even. But be warned...' She fought the urge to either slap or kiss his now teasing, grinning face. 'One mention of virgins, almost or otherwise, and I'm gone.'

CHAPTER FOUR

'ONE RED-HOT RUDOLPH, two Christmas Kisses and a Candy Cane Caipirinha, please.' Poppy shook her head as she gave the order to Isaac. Two hours of cocktail chaos and she was still getting used to the names of these things, and to carrying and fetching.

'Righto, you're getting the hang of this.' He nodded and reached for a bottle of rum. 'I wasn't sure you'd be any use at all.'

'Well, gee, thanks. This may surprise you, but I'm a woman of many talents. Mind you, it is very different from what I'm used to. I'm usually the one giving the orders, so being on the other side of them is a big smack to the ego. Keeping me real.' She did quote marks with her fingers for the *real*. Because nothing kept you more real than assisting at a birth and seeing new life come into being. 'But it's a great crowd. I'm stacking up my good karma points and having fun. Surprisingly.'

Apart from having Isaac's eyes following her around the whole time.

He might well have been just watching to make sure she was doing her job okay, but it felt strange. Intense. She felt scrutinised under his gaze and, every which way she thought about it, she came up wanting. Every sorry experience with him had shown her as an inadequate ingénue, even now after all these years. Had she really blurted out her stupid worries under the influence of way too many wines?

Still, at least the early rush was starting to die down and she could catch her breath. Shame, then, that it only ever seemed to stall when she was around Isaac. 'Clever names. Who came up with them?'

He gave the cocktail-shaker thing a good shake, then poured a bright pink drink into a highball glass, leaned over the bar and popped it on Poppy's tray along with a smaller, salt-rimmed lime-coloured drink. His shirt shifted over his body as he moved, straining across muscles that could not possibly have been honed just by making drinks in a bar. She knew he boxed with Matt and Alex when he was in town, other than that, she realised, she knew very little about his life. Apart from the colour of his boxer shorts. The width of his thighs. And the length... She nearly dropped the tray.

Lost for words, she dragged her eyes away and steadied herself. This was not like her and it was getting out of control.

He didn't seem to notice. 'The whole team had a brainstorming session and came up with the cocktail names. In a couple of weeks we'll be running daily specials on the twelve cocktails of Christmas, so we needed twelve half-decent-sounding ones.'

'That must have been fun. How refreshing to have a job where you can do fun stuff.'

'You don't have a laugh at work?'

'Oh, yes, sometimes, of course. The clients are usually all gorgeous. But this is so...carefree. Making up names for drinks, choosing which music to play, picking out wall colours and decor.'

His eyebrows rose. 'Running an internationally successful business is carefree? Wow, I'd love to see what you mean by intense? Hectic? Challenging?'

'You know what I mean. It's not life and death—and that's just great.' She pigged her eyes at him and enjoyed watching him laugh. 'I love how you've given the clients a couple of recipes to take away and try at home, too. They seem really pleased with that.'

'It always pays to give them an extra something. It's good business.' He pointed at the glasses. 'This is a Christmas Kiss for table two and a Merry Margarita for table six. When you've delivered them you can take a break. The night shift staff are arriving soon so we'll be a little less busy.'

Thank goodness. Being a busy registrar at the hospital was hard enough on her feet, but, despite the fun, waitressing made her back and shoulders hurt, too. She'd have a lot more respect for waitresses in the future. She walked towards what she thought was table six. Had an uncharacteristic mind melt. Was it over in the right corner? Left?

Suddenly a hand clamped round her backside making her jump and nearly lose the glasses onto the floor. 'Hey, little lady. Right in the perfect spot. You looking for someone, because I'm right here. Christmas kiss?'

What? She turned to find a short man with a nasty skin disease, which she'd definitely be looking up in a textbook later, and hair that needed a serious wash, violating her personal space. He reached out for the Merry Margarita and as she watched him she realised she'd been standing under a sprig of mistletoe. The groper grinned. 'These for me? Keep 'em coming.'

'Not unless you're from table six and the last time I looked there were two women sitting there.' She eased her bottom away from his hand. 'Unless you've had a sudden sex change? Or would you like me to give you one? I'm a dab hand with a scalpel.'

He didn't move, but his hand hovered perilously close. 'I was just being friendly. It is the season to be merry.'

'*Jolly.* It's the season to be jolly. Now, walk away from my bottom.' She found him her best sarcastic smile and looked down at his now empty hands. 'Well done. Now, the bar's to your left, the exit to your right. You choose. But any more groping and I'm choosing for you.'

'Well, wow. Nicely done.' This time the voice came from close to her other ear and her bottom remained hands-free. The groper took Isaac's arrival as a sign to head to the bar. 'I was coming over to help—I could see him honing in on your backside from over there. But clearly you have no need for a knight in…' he looked down at his clothes and shrugged '…jeans and a work shirt. Next time I'm looking for a bouncer I'll know where to come.'

He'd come to save her? Cute. Disturbingly sexy. 'Sorry, boss, was I too brutal, out of line? It's just that every Christmas and New Year's Eve there are men like him stalking single women for a quick grope and a snog. The mistletoe's always their excuse. Sad, really.' And, hell, she should know. She was always the one copping the attention from the geek in the corner. And never—never, ever—from someone like Isaac.

'No, you were very in-line. And yet so not the Poppy I know. I'm impressed.' He tugged a hand through his hair. 'So, little mice scare you, but grown men don't? Go figure.'

'I used my work voice. Six months of working in A and E on a Saturday night teaches you how to deal with people who've had too much alcohol…oh.' She felt the blush steal into her cheeks and down her neck. 'I…er…I'm not one to talk.'

'I guess not. You know all about drunken misdemeanours, Dr Spencer. They get you into bed with all the wrong sort of people.' His mouth creased into one of the most breathtaking smiles she'd ever seen. He leaned in close enough that she could smell him. That scent had haunted her all day. His mouth came closer, into full focus... 'Now, about that Christmas kiss...'

'What?' *No.*

Yes. Yes, please! Her body thrilled with a sudden rush of heat, no doubt turning her cheeks from pink to hot Rudolph red. The thought of doing more misdemeanours, preferably with him, and definitely naked, made her hot all over.

Isaac tapped the tray. 'The ice is melting. If you don't get it over to the table soon I'll have to make another one.'

'Of course. Yes. The drink. Right away.' Duh! The cocktail Christmas Kiss. Not the mistletoe. She looked ruefully up at the white berries over her head, shrugging off the shivers of lust skittering down her spine. So inappropriate. Her body screamed disappointment as she watched him walk away. What the hell was happening?

She served the drinks, dodged the groper, removed her apron and headed to the little lounge out back reserved for staff only. Ten minutes would be long enough to get herself together and shake off that weird Isaac-induced vibe.

Okay, so hands up, Izzy was right: there was a vibe. Poppy hadn't really thought of it before, but there was. She'd always felt out of sorts when he was around. Jittery. Nervous. And yet, stupidly anxious to make him see her in a favourable light. There was no one, no one else she ever felt like that with.

In here the seats were the same square, soft, couch types as outside, but the lighting was brighter, making her squint as she walked in. She hadn't been expecting to see Isaac there, kettle in one hand, cup in the other. 'Oh, are you taking a break, too?'

'I was just going to offer you a cuppa, then head upstairs to the office to change the roster now Jamie's likely to be off. It's the least I can do after you've helped me out.' He flicked the kettle on, threw a teabag into a mug. 'Maybe another night you could learn how to make some of the drinks? They'd make your infamous house parties go with a bang.'

'Another night? Not likely, I've done my good Samaritan dash. This was a one-off thing only. I do have a proper job.' Kicking off her shoes, she gave her toes a little massage to ease out the knots and tension. But realised that most of it was coming from inside her gut and not her feet.

Leaning against the counter, he looked relaxed. Easy. In his own space. A direct contrast to how she felt. Getting it together could take a little time. 'I'm well aware of your meteoric rise in the lady-doctoring world, Poppy, and your skills were greatly appreciated here earlier on. Thank you for helping me out with Jamie. But if the challenge ever gets too hard for you and you're just too far out of your *sexperience*-zone...or you just feel like a change of career, there'll always be a place for you here.'

Sexperience? God, beam me up now. 'Hmm, doctor versus barmaid? Tough call.'

He handed her a cup. 'Seriously, I'm grateful you're here. As you can see things get a bit hectic and it'll only get worse as we get closer to Christmas.'

Putting his own drink down, he sat opposite her. No chance of Isaac-free space here. She tried to find some inane non-controversial subject to chat about. 'So are you heading off home for Christmas?'

'Nah.'

'Won't your mum want you home?'

'What? When she has Archie and Henry to fuss over? I don't think so.'

'They're your stepbrothers, right? Won't they want you to be there? Won't you all be doing the Santa Claus thing?' She hoped for their sakes it wouldn't be like the cold, loveless festive time she'd had growing up.

'They will. At eight and six they deserve a decent Christmas.' He shrugged. She'd had the impression he was a little more sympathetic towards his mum now she'd shown she could actually settle down and stay with a man for longer than a few months. Clearly not. He shook his head. 'It's just easier if I stay away.'

'Easier for who?'

Silence stretched between them. He stared into his cup. Eventually his head rose and he met her gaze. 'Easier for us all, to be honest. She has asked me to go down this year for the first time in a long time, but I'm not really into the happy family pretence thing. And since when has my life been of any interest to you?'

Since I kissed you. Saw you half-naked. Almost naked. Lots of bare skin...too much. Not enough.

Since she'd suddenly become overly intrigued by him. 'Just making conversation.'

'Yeah...well.' *Back off.* 'That's weird.'

It was. Yes. But pre-kiss she would have been able to have some kind of conversation with him without thinking about sex. Although clearly not about anything remotely personal to Isaac. Resting her weary feet, she sipped her drink and changed conversational tack. 'I'm surprised you're here doing the actual physical bar work. I imagined you'd have people to do that while you pushed bits of paper around being important.'

'Usually I do—although we're trying to be paper-free so I have to find other ways to look important. But it's early days for this bar and I want to make sure we have the right feel. The only way to do that is to be here when the action happens.'

'And how do you know if you have the right feel? What are you aiming for?'

His eyebrows rose and he carried on chatting, obviously passionate about his work. 'It's hard to quantify. I guess it's more of an instinctive feel. We have a good buzz, the right music and decor. Great service is always important—and, thanks to you, that's happening tonight. Ultimately I'd like this place to be a destination bar like Red and Aqua. Things are going well so far. The takings are brilliant—but then if you can't make a killing in the silly season you're doing something wrong.'

'So how many bars do you have now? Obviously I know about Red, Smoke and…Aqua…in Westbourne Grove, Brixton and…?'

'Newcastle. Five in the UK, six including Bar Gris in Paris. Hopefully one in Amsterdam in the late spring— that's what I was negotiating over there. We have a venue, the fit-out has started. Then it'll be Berlin, possibly New York…'

'And you want more?'

'I always want more, Poppy. Don't you?' His slow smile spread across his face, eyes lighting, too. He shifted forward in his seat, his gaze meeting hers.

Her mouth dried. More? Did he mean what she thought he meant?

Everything had been tipped sideways. But she knew she wanted to touch him again. Definitely more touching.

God, really? Her stomach twisted into a tight knot.

She fancied Isaac? The strange feelings weren't just embarrassment at last night's shenanigans. Or mortification that he knew her deepest truth. She really, truly, bolt-out-of-the-blue wanted him to touch her. Here. Anywhere.

This was not happening.

'Okay, let's get back to work.'

He didn't move an inch but his disconcerting gaze finally left hers and flickered to the back window. 'Ugh, look, it's starting to snow. That'll mean either we get a last rush of punters or they'll all start to leave.'

She ran to the window and watched the tiny swirls of snow, illuminated by the bar's outside lights, falling to the ground. Only a smattering of it had stuck to the pavement, but it was a truly wonderful Christmassy sight. 'Oh, wow, look at that. I love it when it snows.'

He joined her. 'Really? All that sludge and sleet and cold?'

'Scrooge, much? What about making snow angels and snowball fights? Tobogganing? I love it all. We used to sneak out of the boarding house after lights out and have massive snowball fights in the park.'

'Oh, at school? Not target practice with Alex, then?'

'Oh, sure, when we were at home we did, too, but the best fun was at school. Always. Don't you think? Wasn't it for you? I met my closest friends there. And Alex loved it, too—but then it could have been because he wasn't at home. Anything was better than that.'

Isaac shrugged again. His answer for any difficult conversation. But then she realised she'd inadvertently strayed into rocky conversational ground. He'd had to leave boarding school because his parents divorced and his mum couldn't afford to send him any more—meaning he'd enrolled in a local school where he'd allegedly fallen in with a bad crowd. Even though Alex had kept in touch with Isaac, Poppy hadn't seen a lot of him after that. Until the night of her school ball.

The realities of where they stood, what they'd shared, came sharply into focus. He knew her. And she knew him. Knew what his track record with women was like. Knew what he was prepared to give to a relationship and how little that was. Knew he was a lot more experienced than she was and that fact alone scared the hell out of her.

It was one thing to like the look of him, the scent, the feel. But another altogether to even think of anything more.

'Okay, time's up. We should get back to work.' That would be a whole lot better for the both of them.

CHAPTER FIVE

TWO HOURS LATER Isaac watched from the bar as Poppy buttoned up her heavy coat, pulled on a beret-style hat and gloves and tied a scarf around her neck. Instinct made him want to stop her wrapping that gorgeous body up, and then slowly unwrap her, layer by layer. Not just her outer clothes but the ones underneath. To see whether he'd matched the right undies to the right girl. And then to get another glimpse of her clothesless body. To shed layer after layer of the pretence they'd lived with for years—the unspoken scenario that had kept them at arm's length—and see more of the real woman. He'd glimpsed that, too, the other night—amazing how alcohol could lower a person's guard. She was successful, professional and yet vulnerable. Lost and naive. And ever since their conversation in the staff lounge she'd been detached, too.

Interesting. As was the sharp sting of lust every time he got a whiff of her scent. Which meant he really did need a little geographical distance.

She gave him a weak smile, or at least he thought she did—he couldn't really tell as her mouth was hidden by the layers of wool round her neck. Her voice was muffled. 'I'm heading off now. I'll see you at home?'

He'd be in Alex's bad books for ever if he let his sister walk the snowy London streets on her own at this time of night. He figured offering to ride home with her might get a more favourable response to offering her just a ride. 'Wait, I'll come with you.'

'It's okay. I'll be fine.' She walked towards the door.

He finished wiping down the counter tops, flicked on the dishwasher. 'I know that you'll be fine, but if you can wait for a few minutes while I close up we can go together. It seems stupid to trudge all that way on your own for the sake of a couple of minutes. Or are you in a hurry for some reason?'

After a couple of seconds' thought she came back and leaned on the bar counter. 'You know very well that I have nothing to get back for, or to get up for tomorrow. I get a lie-in until the week after next if I want to.'

'Strange way to spend a holiday if you ask me.' Although spending a week in bed with Poppy could be very interesting indeed.

And this was the guy trying to avoid those kind of thoughts.

She gave him a smile that lit up her face. 'Why, Big Shot Bar Man? What rates as a good holiday for you?'

'Not staying in my flat in London on my own in the cold, for a start. I'd prefer surfing somewhere, travelling around South America, exploring new places.' Roots weren't something he craved. Home wasn't a place he'd had much experience of for quite a few years.

'Sounds wonderful, if I ever got the chance. Travelling is on my bucket list, but there's a lot of medical training to get through first.' She huffed out a breath. 'I can't afford to go anywhere, so there it is. I'm planning a couple of days shopping for presents. Chilling out a lot. And Izzy said she'd come ice-skating with me. That'll be fun.'

'Geez, yes. More cold. I bet you love Christmas, too.'

'Don't you?'

'I'd love a South African Christmas, or surfing at Bondi.

That way I don't have to think about all that…mushy sentimental stuff.'

'What, family and friends and being together?'

'Yeah.'

'And now you're Scrooge, too. Who the hell have I let into my flat? Don't let your night-time visitors from Christmas past keep me awake with their clanking chains. I have enough to contend with, with those damned mice.' She tutted and laughed but hung around until he'd dragged down the shutters and locked up. Then slid into step with him towards the Angel Islington tube station. The road was eerily quiet, the snow deadening their steps. Thick dark clouds above threatened more snow as tiny flakes fluttered around them. Walking alongside Poppy in such an ethereal landscape gave him a strange kick beneath his ribcage. Okay, he had to admit, it looked nice. But it was nothing to get excited about.

'Aw, come on, don't tell me you don't like this? It's like magic.' She caught a snowflake on her tongue and stuck it out at him. 'Yum.'

His gaze lingered on her mouth as he thought about all the things that tongue could do, then he shook his head minutely. Once again it was late, he was tired—he didn't need the whole 'wanting Poppy' thing going on. Although, his body obviously had different ideas. Bad ideas. Good bad ideas. In hindsight he should have let her go home on her own, but what self-respecting man would let a woman walk the streets of London on her own in a snowstorm?

Although, judging by her dealings with the groper, she'd probably fare pretty well. Annoying little pre-pubescent Poppy had turned into a surprisingly strong woman. 'It's weather, Poppy. Not magic. You're the scientist, surely you should know that.'

'And you're the least romantic person I've ever met. And I don't mean cutesy, soppy, happy-ever-after stuff—I mean deep, wondrous, meaningful, secrets-of-the-universe stuff. Nature makes these amazing things.'

'You've been spending too much time with loved-up Izzy.'

She did an irritated eye roll. 'Where's your heart and soul? Can't you see past reality and dream a little?'

'Dreams? Romance? Hello? Where's the scientist gone?' Romance was for bleeding hearts. He'd never been into the wooing gig. Never found a woman he'd wanted to spend much time on, to be honest. What he knew about women, to date, was that most of them got turned on by a platinum credit card. His mother included, it seemed, with her relentless pursuit of richer, younger, better.

He hadn't needed, or cared enough, to worry about anything past that. 'Dream about what exactly? Ice particles melting on my *filiform papillae*?' At her impressed eyebrow-raise he grinned. 'You weren't the only one who aced biology. But it's a strange thing to get soppy about.'

'It's way more than just melting ice, Isaac. Each snowflake has a unique pattern created depending on specific humidity and temperature of the atmosphere. Made at cloud level, and not, as some think, as they fall to earth.' Aaand…there was the scientist. Hallelujah. 'Oh, and they look pretty.'

And…gone again. 'Huh? *Magical.* If you like that kind of thing.'

'How can you not? You've got to take time out to enjoy the small stuff.' Seemed the life philosophising wasn't just restricted to a drunken stage—she was at a point in her life when she was questioning what it was all about. He got that. Occasionally he looked at what he'd achieved and wondered if that was it. Six bars, a very healthy bank account and a penthouse apartment. The sum total of his life, which was pretty full and, some would say, very successful. But when he looked deeper he recognised that just maybe there was something missing, too.

He chose not to dwell on that.

They reached the station and began the long process of descending deep into the underground. She stood in front of him as the first escalator moved slowly south. He could see her profile; snowflakes dusted her hair, eyelashes, the tip of her nose. Now that was the kind of licking off melting ice he could live with. Her nose crinkled as she spoke. 'You've seen lots of romance around you—don't you think some might have rubbed off a bit? How long have you lived in our flat and how many chick flicks have you watched?'

'Not watched, endured. As few as possible. Why do you think I spend so much of my time at work?' One mention of a chick flick and he'd always left. Just one downside of living with a bunch of women.

'So what do you dream about?'

He thought back to lying in her bed—in those half-moments between being asleep and awake—and the sudden hitch in his breathing as he'd watched her, the strange unexpected emotion, the need to protect her, to hold her. Not that he'd wanted to make love with her then, because he would never have taken a woman who wasn't in any state to remember it, or who would regret it the instant it was over. But he'd thought about what sex with her might be like...some time. One time. Oh, yes, a man *could* dream—just not the kind of dreaming she meant. 'Believe me, sweetheart, you don't want to know.'

She stared up at him, for a second, two. Three. His peripheral vision closed down and all he could see was her face, those shining cautious eyes, pink cheeks. That mouth that he wanted to cover with his own. There was something about her, beyond attractive, something bone-deep that intrigued him. She wasn't the person he'd thought she was. She was different, matured, strong but yet innocent.

She gave him a very shy and very faint smile. 'Maybe I do, Isaac.'

At least that was what he thought she said. Before he could clarify she'd turned away, almost running down the second escalator without looking back. And he let her go, because he clearly wasn't the only one confused as all hell, and turned on, to boot.

She eventually stopped to work out the correct platform. 'This one?'

'Sure. Now, don't go too close to the edge.'

'Aww, that's kind. But I've been riding the tube for a long time. I know the drill.'

He laughed. 'Kind? Not really...well, not to you, anyway. I just saw a mouse running along the side of the track and I didn't want you to give it a heart attack with your banshee screaming. Poor thing, minding its own business. It doesn't deserve that.'

'There are always mice or rats in these kinds of places. I came to terms with that a long time ago. I just don't like them in my house. Under my couch. Or my bed.' She closed her eyes and he just knew she was drawing on some kind of inner strength. But she edged a little closer to the platform edge and he almost wrapped an arm round her. For the sake of mouse protection. But stopped himself.

She was having a strange effect on him. Last night as she'd told him about her insecurities at work and her sexual inexperience he'd felt a mix of rage and...empathy. She'd guilted herself, limited her own personal growth because of the actions of one selfish, stupid man who had used his position of power to hurt her. Isaac surprised himself by genuinely wanting to make her feel better.

That was strange.

He read out the LED display to distract himself, wanting to get away from any more deep and meaningful. It freaked him out. 'Two minutes until the next train.'

'Yep. What'll we talk about?'

He looked up and down the platform. At the far end there were two guys sitting on a bench. That was it, no one in any kind of proximity. He scrabbled around trying to find something to lighten the tone. 'I could fill in a few gaps in your knowledge for you, if you like?'

She frowned. 'What do you mean?'

'Last night you told me you feel a little…er…unprepared for some of the answers to your clients' questions? What exactly do you need to know?' Okay, so distraction therapy wasn't working.

Her eyes did a funny widening popping thing. Not necessarily a positive reaction. 'I beg your pardon? You want to talk dirty to me?'

'If you say so. What is it about sex that you need to learn? I can help. Either a nice quiet chat where I fill in the gaps—or, I could do the whole show and tell thing. Your choice.'

'As if I'd ask you.' But she didn't deny she wanted to learn. What he could see of her cheeks bloomed bright red.

'Hey, you did me a huge favour tonight. So go on. Ask. Ask me anything. I can pay you back in answers. And I pinky promise I won't laugh.' He held out his little finger.

Shoving her hands deep into her pockets, she squared up to him. 'Just forget whatever I said last night, okay? I was rambling and drunk. I don't need to learn anything. I'm quite capable of understanding the mechanics. I'm doing obstetrics—believe me, I know where babies come from.'

'Okay. Whoa, call off the cavalry. I'm sorry.'

The train arrived and they clambered on, took a seat in a carriage where they were the only people. Even so, she kept her voice a low hiss. 'You have the problem with sex, Isaac. Not me. How long has your longest relationship been? A month? Thirty whole days?'

He really regretted bringing this up. It had been a joke. But, 'Hey, I can't help it if I'm in it for the long haul.'

Her eyes widened again. 'You think long haul is a month?'

'It isn't? Really? That's where I've been going wrong?' He laughed. 'I have no problem with sex. None at all. But commitment is seriously overrated.'

'Men. Typical bloody men.' She sighed. This time it wasn't soft and sleepy; it was downright narky. And it told him to back right off.

And there was the fundamental issue. Poppy believed sex and relationships had to be intertwined, inextricably linked, which was probably why she'd backed away from any hint of any since her first disastrous relationship. Whereas he made sure he only ever dated women who wanted a little harmless fun and relaxation.

The train finally rattled to a stop and they disembarked, lungs filling with the thick metal smell of the underground air. She stomped off ahead and, once out of the station, stalked off through the snow, arms crossed over her body, a niggly line on her forehead.

'Poppy, wait. Come on, it was a joke.'

'Ha-bloody-ha.' She quickened her pace.

As they stomped he scuffed his hand along the top of a wall and collected enough snow to form a snowball. Then stopped and grabbed his ankle. 'Ouch. Ouch.'

'What's the matter?' Bingo. She turned, ran back to him. God forgive him, he almost felt guilty. But not enough. She bent to look at his leg, all concerned and serious. 'What is it?'

'It's a ball made up of pretty magical unique ice crystals. Apparently.' He stuffed it into the collar of her coat. 'Gotcha.'

She screamed. Shivered. Turned. 'What the…? You are the most irritating, stupid, insensitive…' Chasing after him, scooping snow as she ran, she threw a hard ball at his back, the smile finding its way back onto her mouth. 'One more time, Isaac, and I swear...'

He threw one back at her. Missed by a mile. On purpose. 'What? You love snowball fights? What you going to do? Go on. I dare you.'

She threw another one. It lamely hit his leg. He ran and caught her up, reached out for her arm, grabbed it.

She spun around in the snow, dark eyes flashing with anger, frustration.

Heat. It slammed through him like a thousand volts as he touched her.

Her body shook and she glanced down, surprised, at her trembling hands. Looked up at him for answers. He didn't have any. He didn't know what the hell was happening here either.

Her voice was thick and hoarse. 'No. No. You're not worth it.'

'Oh, really?' The electric force that had shimmied between them all evening spiked, stole his breath. He pulled her to him, slamming his body against hers. He needed to kiss her. To taste her again. Because one tiny kiss had been in no way enough last night.

If she had given him any indication that she did not want this as much as he did then he would have walked. But she kept staring at him, searching his face. Confused. Hungry.

'Really. You are so not worth it. Not worth it at all.' But this time her voice was hushed and thick and told him exactly what he needed to know.

He watched the movement of her throat as she swallowed, brushed a snowflake from her cheek. 'Poppy...'

'Yes?' She stuck her tongue out again and caught another one, smiled in a way that shot hot spikes of need through him. Ran her tongue along her top lip leaving a wet trail that he ached to taste, and half drove him mad with desire. Her eyes widened and he was sure she didn't realise the effect she was having on him. Either she had to stop or he had to… 'You have got to stop doing that with your tongue.'

'Why?' Her breathing sped up, her lips parted just a little.

He tipped his head closer to her mouth, unable to do anything else but stand here, with her, holding her. 'Because I have other ideas for it.'

Poppy heard the catch in her throat and felt the shiver run the length of her body as he pulled her to him by her coat lapels, pushed away her scarf and slid his mouth over hers. Felt her body ease against his. Felt the thick outlines of his heavy coat against hers—frustrated by the barriers. Grateful for the barriers.

Because she knew they were on different planets of experience, of expectation. She didn't want to kiss him. Didn't want to want him.

But she did. She wanted him to run his hands over her body. Wanted to see what it felt like to feel desirable, to *be* desirable, to Isaac.

And hell, she needed to stop hiding, stop processing. Start living. Start feeling—but she didn't know how. She wanted him to show her the way, but was afraid of what he'd think of her. And she sure as hell couldn't ask.

As he slowly licked across her bottom lip, any further thought fled her brain. Her body stopped processing anything beyond its innate feral response; the flashes of light and heat in her belly, the tingle in her breasts, the wet of her mouth.

She opened her mouth, unable to resist the pull of him any more, wound her arms around his neck. Felt a strip of bare skin against her arm—that one inch enough to fire more light. More heat. Lost herself in touch, smell. Taste.

And man, he tasted good. Of sin and sex. Of chaos. Of ice and snow and fire and heat. It was an open-mouthed kiss—gentle. Soft. Not greedy or sloppy, as she'd had all those years ago. Not rushed or panting.

His hands cupped her face, as she'd seen on the movies, as she'd seen other couples do—no rampant groping or grasping. No sweaty hands pulling at her clothes. No guilt suffusing every touch. No hurry. No hiding.

Surprising. Delicious. Fresh. Unsullied heat swirled inside her, prickling all her nerve endings, making her feel alive.

But despite the tenderness he was still all male. Confident. Giving. Taking. Making her insides melt away along with her resolve. His tongue slipped into her mouth and at first she didn't know how to react. Too much, too little. Too hard. Not hard enough. A hot rock of panic began to rise from her gut. He was too much for her. She wasn't enough for him.

But gently, gently he coaxed her tongue, stroking, probing, dancing. And she realised she was rocking against him, greedy to feel the contours of his body. Wondering how it would feel to have him inside her.

No.

Whoa.

She pulled away. Those kinds of thoughts made her blood pressure enter the critical range. Memories of destruction roiled back. The last time she'd allowed herself to get carried away she'd almost destroyed too many lives. And even though the logical part of her brain knew that this time there were only two people at stake here—she wasn't prepared to put herself in the firing line. Not with Isaac.

God. Why the hell couldn't she just let go a little? Have the fun she craved? She wanted it. She did.

But eight years of cutting herself off from any kind

of sexual feeling wasn't easy to shrug off. And when she did finally let herself go it had to be on equal terms. She didn't want to feel like a loser, or in any way inadequate.

If she was ever going to have any kind of relationship, which was not on the cards right now, she had to know what she was doing, so she could choose, could have a say in what happened next. She had to have something to offer, and right now she didn't. She was at risk and she didn't like that. Not at all. 'Isaac. Sorry. I…I can't. This isn't me. I don't do this. I need to go home. I'm sorry.'

He stared back at her, confusion written across his features.

He was every kind of wrong. And he knew it, too. Snow turning to cold, damp sleet fell on his shoulders. Down her neck, onto her face. And she began to shiver. He let her go, his breath rushing into the cold night air. 'Crap, Poppy. That wasn't meant to happen.'

'No. It wasn't.' She shoved her hands back into her pockets, ignored the sting of her swollen lips and headed home. Annoyed, frustrated and wondering how the hell she was going to survive until February with him living in her apartment with a *vibe* that was almost palpable.

Mice. Vibes. Isaac. So much for being lonely. The apartment was getting way too full for her liking.

CHAPTER SIX

THE ONLY WAY Poppy was going to get through the department Christmas party was to immerse herself in having a good time. She would chat to everyone. She might even dip her toe into some very gentle flirting if there was a suitable man around. Definitely very gentle.

At the very least, she would try. Try to put the kiss behind her. Try to do what every normal woman her age did—go out with men, brave the waters. Garner a little sexual experience. With all her friends coupled off she needed something fresh to inject into her life, and a date for Izzy's wedding—although turning up single wouldn't be the worst thing she could ever do.

Or the best.

But it would be nice to have someone to share this kind of thing with. Someone safe. Someone who wouldn't stomp on her heart. Who wouldn't lie and cheat. Or, who wouldn't be incapable of giving more than thirty days if that was what they decided they wanted. Together.

A nice reliable doctor perhaps. Suitable. Unlike Isaac. Very unsuitable.

And that would just about give her friends a heart attack! Poor Poppy who had never been seen with so much as a sniff of a man on her arm finally braving the dating waters.

Or was she living in cloud cuckoo land?

She looked across Blue private room, all a-sparkle with sophisticated blue and silver Christmas decorations, which gave the place a mystical feel, and watched as her Obs and Gynae team relaxed into the Christmas spirit—some more than others.

'He's had a few too many Christmas kisses, don't you think?' Tim, the specialist registrar, pointed over to Prof Hartley, obstetrician to royalty and the stars, slumped in a corner, his nose as red as Santa's suit.

Poppy laughed at the prospect of the almost-seventy-year-old under the mistletoe. Or downing the now infamous cocktail. Either seemed a stretch for the big guy. 'In his dreams.'

'And, judging by the snoring, I imagine he's having plenty of them. This is a great party. Well done.'

'Thanks. We managed to pull it out of the hat, I think.' High praise indeed. Pride rippled through her—although she hadn't had much of a hand in prepping for the event. Isaac had sorted out most of the details and left enquiring and confirming notes on the kitchen counter. Or sent short texts.

Fish of the day? Salmon okay?

Yes. Fine.

DJ or just MP3?

MP3.

Champagne or Aussie bubbles?

Cheapest?

She got the feeling he'd been avoiding her as much as she'd been avoiding him.

Where was she? Oh, yes. Tim.

'Do you want another drink?' Tim looked harmless enough. In fact, he was quite attractive, in an understated kind of way. He was quite funny, clever, en route to being a very successful doctor. He had a fairly hot body. Unobtrusive dress sense. And was back on the dating scene after a five-year relationship break-up with a woman who had run off with her dentist a few months ago. He would be a definite catch for someone looking to start dating again. He was stable, had good prospects and made her laugh.

And he seemed quite interested in more than just a drink, judging by the way he'd hung around with her for most of the evening, 'catching up'. She only hoped he wasn't quite a good kisser but a damned fine one. Because he'd need to be if she was going to erase Isaac from her mind.

'I'd love one. Thanks. Just a sparkling water.' Because Lord knew what effect anything stronger would have on her.

'You're being very professional, but you can let your hair down at the end-of-year party, you know. No one will judge you. How about you have just one cocktail?' He had a nice voice, too. Quite calming. Slight northern accent. Pleasant enough. Just not enough to make her heart trip. Maybe he'd grow on her. He looked to be just the type of man she could manage.

'No, thanks.' Cocktails would for ever only remind her of Isaac.

'Go on. I'll grab the menu for you.' Tim leaned across her to the table, accidentally catching her arm. 'Oh, sorry.'

'No problem.' It was just skin on skin. Plain old skin. No problem. No tingles either. 'But seriously, I'm fine with water.'

Maybe he was perfect for her.

'Yes, water is best. You do not want to see her when she's drunk.' That voice again. Her heart jittered. She turned and saw Isaac standing next to her, an old T-shirt skimming muscles that had haunted her dreams. Faded jeans and work boots completing a picture that made her feel very unsafe indeed. And he was grinning that heart-stopping grin that told her he knew he was being a giant pain in the ass, but didn't give a damn.

And hell, if that kiss didn't linger between them now, filling the air with an electricity so intense she felt her lungs empty.

But, if anything, Isaac's entrance certainly cemented Tim as a possible contender. Tim wouldn't leave her lungs empty, or her unmentionables zinging.

She looked back at her colleague, who was smiling, earnestly holding out the menu to her. She took it, ignoring Isaac. Trying to ignore him.

'Why?' Tim turned to Isaac again, his smile fading. 'What is she like?'

Don't say another damned word, buster. But polite was necessary, especially in front of a potential date. 'Oh. Isaac, perfect timing, I didn't see you come in.' Which was mighty strange considering her eyes had been fixed on the door for most of the evening. She spoke through gritted teeth. 'Tim, this is Isaac, an old friend of my brother's. He owns this bar, plus he's my flatmate.'

'Isaac.' Tim stretched out his hand. 'Nice to meet you.'

'Tim.' There was no *nice*. There was, however, a hint of a glower.

And why that gave her a tingling feeling she didn't want to know.

Tim's smile resurrected. 'Thanks for letting us have the bar at such short notice. I know Poppy was very relieved. I hope it didn't put you out too much.'

Oh, good. Tim was polite, too. Another tick.

He leaned in a little closer. Territorial? She got a whiff of his not-unpleasant cologne. Saw his passable jaw in profile. Yes. He was nice. Her heart sank a little.

Trouble was, Tim might well be someone's perfect catch but so far he just wasn't hers. There was no magic. No frisson of electricity. No zinging.

Basically, she didn't want to jump his bones. Which was a shame—because they were probably quite nice, unobtrusive bones, underneath his corduroy trousers and check shirt.

The other trouble was, jumping bones wasn't something she was very adept at.

And there she was over-analysing everything again.

Go with the flow. Magic could grow. She hadn't wanted to jump Isaac's bones for what…twenty years…and that seemed to have just grown out of nowhere. Inconveniently.

Isaac's grin lingered, as if he knew exactly what storm he was causing in her gut. 'Oh, fitting you in was no trouble at all. We had a vacant slot so we were happy to help your department out. Besides, Poppy has a very unique way of convincing a man to do her bidding. We're all powerless to resist.' Isaac patted Tim on the back and then leaned in. 'A word of warning, though. She's a hell of a snorer.'

With that he walked away.

Mortified, Poppy gave Tim a weak smile and shrugged. 'We have thin walls.'

'Thin…?' Tim watched as Isaac sauntered towards the bar. 'Is there anything…you know…between…you two?'

'Me and Isaac? No way.' Why did that have a ring to it? Second time this week she'd denied anything between her and Isaac. Going by the 'repeat it enough and you'll start to believe it' mantra she answered, 'No. There's nothing. He's just my flatmate.'

But she was damned sure you didn't follow *just* your flatmate's backside as he walked away. Didn't spend hours in bed waiting for *just* your flatmate to leave so you wouldn't bump into him and try to kiss him again. And, hell, you never thought about *just* your flatmate naked when you heard him in the shower.

She fired imaginary daggers at Isaac's back. Trust him to come along and spoil her attempt at a relaxed night out. Now she'd have to take a zillion deep breaths and cool off before she could restart her operation fun campaign. With Tim.

She turned back to him, and he held out a glass of water, which she rolled across her chest to try to get some relief. He gave her a startled stare and she realised she hadn't ever thought about him naked. Which surely must be a good sign. 'Now, about that drink?'

Isaac had had enough. Exhaustion ate away at him along with something else that he didn't want to put a name to. But he was damned sure seeing Poppy getting friendly with a *pretty decent chap* might be up there as culprit number one.

Add to the five almost sleepless nights where he couldn't shrug off the unease about kissing Poppy, *twice*, and enjoying it; he was damned well going to sleep tonight if it was the last thing he did.

Shoving the key in the lock, he entered the flat as quietly as he could, relieved that the place was in darkness. He hung up his coat, silently placed his briefcase on the floor, slipped off his boots and—

'You're very late.'

At the sound of Poppy's voice his heart ramped up to a thousand beats a minute. 'Poppy. You made me jump. Not that it's any of your business, but I was closing up and helping some old professor guy get safely home.' All of which he'd prolonged, unsure of how he'd feel coming home and finding Poppy in a clinch with Troy…? Terry…? In the apartment. Worse, if he'd heard things happening in the bed he'd shared with her not many nights ago. Not that it would be any of his business. Not that he would ever have a claim on her. Although, currently, the prospect of seeing her and not touching her was driving him a little crazy. He could only hope it would dissipate and normal service would be resumed. A state where he wasn't über-conscious of her every move, laugh, word. 'Had a good night?'

'Until you came along. Yes.' She was sitting on the couch. His heart steadied. Well, almost. Fully clothed, as far as he could see—his night vision hadn't quite focused yet. Wearing, for the record, a far-too-sexy black dress that skimmed her breasts and her backside and had made every man in that room want her. Shoes with heels that made her legs model-long and very sexy indeed. And her dark hair piled on her head, with swirls of curls around her face. She'd highlighted her eyes with a smoky grey liner and eye make-up that shimmered. *Shimmered.* With lipstick that drew any sensible bloke's attention to her lips. Way too sexy for a Friday night. Or any night that had a Y in it.

But no clinch. No man. He exhaled, deeply. 'Why? What did I do?'

'*We're powerless to resist her.* And…*she snores.*' Poppy snorted. 'Gee, thanks. If that wasn't enough to put him off I don't know what was.'

'If he doesn't want you because you snore then he isn't the man for you. Because, well—face it, you might as well hand out ear plugs.' He looked around the room. 'Where is he, anyway?'

'Turns out, he wasn't the man for me.'

'Like we didn't all know that. But he was very…' He tried to think of the worst insult he could find. The guy had seemed pretty decent. Just so not Poppy's type. Which was? Hell if he knew. He didn't even want to think about it. And she definitely was not anywhere on *his* list of types. But the only thing he could think of was that holding her and kissing her had seemed so far beyond… 'Nice.'

'Yes…he is, very…nice. And that's not a bad thing. I like nice. And safe. And slow. And predictable. And open to commitment. And he's just been in a five-year relationship. Five years, imagine that.'

'And it ended?' Isaac raised his palms towards her. 'Proves my point.'

'Which is?'

'Nothing is for ever.'

'Not if you don't give it a chance. Wait until you find The One. You'll see. What about Alex and Lara? Izzy and Harry? Tori and Matt?'

'They all just got lucky.' He didn't want to add that he'd given himself a silent bet that Izzy would leave Harry at the altar. Alex and Lara wouldn't be talking to each other when they got back from holiday. And Matt and Tori would break up before they even got to South Africa.

'Lucky? It happens to be called love—and they all seem pretty happy about it. Even those who took a bit of convincing.'

Did Poppy just want to be like her friends? All coupled up? 'And I can show you plenty of evidence that love doesn't last, not once there's a roadblock, or the slightest hint of trouble ahead.' Starting with his mother, and…his mother…and his mother…

'You know, your mum seems very happy, currently. And settled. She's been married to Hugo a long time now. See, it is possible to find someone and something that lasts.'

And that was a swift punch to his gut. How did Poppy know he was thinking…? 'Until the next time.'

'You need to cut her some slack. It can't have been easy thinking she was falling in love and then realising and admitting she'd made a mistake. It must have been hard for her, extricating herself from a situation she didn't want to be in. Being less than perfect in front of her son. At least, I couldn't imagine my mum ever admitting she was in the wrong.'

And he hadn't ever looked at it like that. The way his mother had kept him in the dark about her love life had left him reluctant to turn up at yet another one of her weddings. It wasn't as if she'd exactly poured her heart out to him but she'd always seemed happy at first. And she'd never, ever said she'd made a mistake about love. She'd made it all sound as if it was more about cash flow. But then, Poppy could have read it wrong, too—she wasn't exactly famous for her good judge of character.

Which probably explained why she'd tried to kiss him in the first place.

Poppy twiddled one of the straps on her barely-there dress as her speech sped up and her voice rose. 'So, I don't know what your game is, Isaac, but you can butt right out of my social life.'

'I didn't invite myself to be in it in the first place. If I remember rightly it was you. You asked to use my bar. You started all this.' He didn't need to say 'you kissed me...' but it hovered there in the silence.

'Yes, well. Let's finish it.' She clicked on a side lamp, flooding the room with washed orange light. Goddamn, he wished she hadn't. Because sitting there in that dress, her hair half up, half down, mouth still slicked with lipstick, pouting. Pouting, for God's sake. She looked bed-ready. Sex-ready.

'I don't need you sussing out my potentials, Isaac.'

'Potentials?' She was thinking about dating someone else? Goddamn. He didn't want to think about how that made him feel. *Not your business.* But a tight fist of something speared him in the gut.

'Yes. Potentials. I don't want you frightening them off. I don't want you talking to them, okay? And while we're at it, I think we need a few house rules for while you're here. I don't want you walking around the flat half naked any more. Keep those boxer shorts out of plain sight. Okay?'

He looked down. Huh? Just shirt, jeans and socks very definitely on show. 'My boxer shorts?'

'Yes.'

He stifled a laugh, figuring she wouldn't take kindly to that. Poor little Poppy might be sussing out potentials, but was having a hard time controlling her libido with him. All it would take would be one little spark…

So, he would not be going there. At all. 'Okay. No boxers on show. That works for me, but only if you keep your fancy underwear under wraps. No more knickers and bras on the bathroom radiator. And those pink pyjama things… anywhere.'

She frowned. 'My pyjamas?'

He looked at those shapely shoulders, the skin that he'd run his fingers over, that he knew felt like soft silk. 'Yes. They're too…bed-like. Always wear a dressing gown.'

'Fine.' She shrugged.

So did he. 'Fine.'

'Then, goodnight.' She stood and walked barefoot to the bathroom, slammed the door and turned the radio on. Loud.

Which was a good job because then she wouldn't hear him wince as he thought about her undressing. About what he knew he was missing. And about what he knew he could never have.

CHAPTER SEVEN

LATER—MUCH, MUCH LATER—a wild scream dragged Isaac from a fitful sleep. *WTF?*

Heart thumping almost out of his chest, he jumped from his bed and ran to the lounge, stopping only briefly to pick up a softball bat from behind his door.

'Poppy! Poppy, are you okay? What the hell?'

This time the lights were on and she stood on the couch shivering in those damned pink pyjamas, and, let it be duly noted, no dressing gown...her face pale, her hair messy and knotty at the back, eyes sleep-filled. She pointed to the corner of the skirting board and the small grey plastic box. 'There...there...it's a mouse. In the trap. A mouse.'

'A mouse? Is that all?' An ill-concealed expletive left his lips as he inhaled deeply, filling his lungs with chilly air and Poppy's sweet scent. This woman was responsible for other people's lives? Still, at least she was safe. Thank God. 'Okay, the mouse is captured and can't get out. The trap worked exactly like we hoped. There are no murderers in the flat. All is good.' Not laughing was hard. Stopping himself from hauling her into his arms was a lot harder. 'So, we screamed loudly enough to wake the whole damned neighbourhood, because...?'

'I heard a scratching noise so I got up. I saw the mouse moving around. It made me jump. I screamed. So sue me.'

She peered at the bat in his hand. 'And you think I'm over-reacting. You were planning to do what with that?'

'I thought that the only possible explanation for your blood-curdling screams was that you were being attacked by at least five burglars.'

'And you thought you could fight them off? Sweet. Delusional, but sweet.'

'Hey, honey, I have a lot of expensive stuff. I didn't want them nicking it.' Truth was, he'd become seriously unstuck at the thought of her being hurt and hadn't stopped to think about what might have happened. All he'd known was that for some annoying reason every cell in his body was duty bound to protect her. He held out his hand and tried to talk her down from the soft furnishings. 'Come and say hello to the nice housemate. He won't bite. Or escape.'

'Not likely. No chance.' She looked at his hand and shook her head. 'Just get rid of him.'

'Absolutely. Tomorrow.' Then he realised it already was tomorrow. 'Later. Right now I'm going to try to get some sleep. Please only scream if there is a real emergency. I'm talking blood or fire, okay? Anything else can wait.'

He turned and started to go back to bed.

Her voice made him stop. He was coming to realise that a lot about her made a lot of him stop...his heart, his brain. 'Wait. Isaac. You're not seriously thinking you can leave him here? Like that? He might escape. He might hurt himself.'

'What exactly would you like me to do at silly o'clock?'

'Take him outside? Let him go?'

'It's the middle of the night! The information leaflet said we had to take him at least a mile away and put him in a field with long grass. I'm not walking in Holland Park at this hour, in the snow. Not even for you.' He was surprised to think that he might like to do something for her…to please her. But not this. At her frown he relented slightly. 'Tomorrow. Morning. Okay?'

'Well, if you won't take him, I will. Now.'

No way would he let her, but he wanted to tease her just a little more. 'This I've got to see. You can't even look at him, never mind pick him up. Go on…try.'

She bit her bottom lip, but didn't budge. 'You can't leave him in here.'

'Then I'll put him in my room.'

'Thank you.' She rubbed her eyes sleepily and he found himself mesmerised by the movement of her hands. When she stopped, hands still framing her face, she looked at him, really looked at him. Her gaze roved his face, then his shirtless body, his waist. Lower. And he saw the exact moment when her eyes misted. Her voice was husky and fractured as she spoke and he didn't think it was down to sleep deprivation. 'Hey, the boxers. I thought we agreed? Violating the agreement so soon?'

'I was trying to be the hero. Strangely, fulfilling the flatmate dress code wasn't top of my to-do list.' He flicked the waistband at his hip. 'So, what to do? Punish me? Or do you want me to take them off? Hey, do you want to take them off? Because we should also have an equal opportunities policy, too.'

Her eyes grew wide. 'No way. No. Fully clothed. More clothes, please. More. Clothes.'

He pointed to her body. 'And what's with the pyjamas? We agreed. Although, I won't have the same reaction if you offer to take them off…and I could help. Just putting it out there.'

Her pupils darkened and her lips parted just enough. Then, after she clearly internally debated the pros and cons of having him butt naked in the lounge, she shook her head and pointed to his room. 'Go to bed. I'll see you tomorrow.'

'Okay.' He grinned and walked away, relieved that she'd

had the sense to put a stop to this…this delicious, sensuous game of human cat and mouse, because he had a feeling he was at risk of getting caught, too. 'Goodnight. Get
some decent sleep. We have some serious mouse releasing tomorrow.'

'Wait. Isaac?'

'Yes?' Second thoughts? His mouth dried. What little
sense had been there before evaporated.

'The mouse?'

Damn. He'd forgotten. He turned, made the few strides
over to her and discovered she'd braved enough to peer
closer at the box.

'I'll just—' He bent to pick it up but en route his hand
banged against hers. She grasped it, whether to steady
herself he didn't know, but a shot of raw electricity ripped
through him. It was as if he'd gripped a thousand-volt wire.
And he couldn't let go.

From this vantage point he was looking down at the top
of her head. Noticed the slight tremor running through her
body and wondered if she was having the same thoughts
and sensations he was. Was she fighting and failing? He
noticed, too, that she hadn't turned to look up at him.

Hadn't? Couldn't? Wouldn't?

He needed to let her go. Double quick before they did
something they'd both regret.

'Isaac?' Finally she tilted her head, stood up and faced
him, her hand still in his. Stepped closer. Raised on her
tiptoes, and with her other hand she cupped his cheek,
pulled his face closer.

Before he could register what she was doing, what she
was asking, what this meant, she'd covered his mouth with
hers.

Oh, my God. Her body had begun to shake and she couldn't
stop. She'd kissed him again. No surprises there, because

the past few days that was all she'd been able to think about. In contrast, Tim's nice attempt at a doorstep kiss had left her cold, which was when she'd explained to him that they needed to keep things platonic.

Platonic.

If only she could feel that about her flatmate, if only she weren't walking into temptation every single time she was here with him alone. But he smelt so good. Tasted so good. And right now those infamous boxers were not concealing how turned on he was. All that rolled up in a guy hell-bent on being her hero, if only for a very short amount of time, made him very appealing indeed. She pulled him to the sofa.

His hands stroked down her back and every inch of Poppy's body strained for his touch. He took too long to reach under her pyjama top and cup her breast. So she undid the buttons, took his hand and placed it there ignoring the flare of concern in his eyes. She wanted him to touch her.

And he did. Which made her stomach tighten and a moan escape her throat. Her nipples beaded as he ran slow circles round them with his fingertips.

'You are so damned gorgeous, Poppy. But slow down a little, eh?' Then his mouth followed his fingers, sucking each nipple, lapping his hot, wet tongue against her skin. Sensation after sensation rippled through her and she bucked against him. She wanted to feel everything. To do everything. To make up for lost time and the last eight years of celibacy. It couldn't be shrugged off quickly enough. She wanted him. Wanted Isaac to show her what she'd been missing.

He took too long to lick back along to her neck. She wanted him now. Pressure built inside her until she felt she was going to explode. She pressed greedily against him relishing his heat and the hardness just inches away from her sweet spot. Her hands twitched to touch him. There. To stroke him. There. To feel him. There.

It wasn't as if she even had to undress him. There was barely a barrier between them. Just those damn boxers.

Should she do something to move him along a little? Her one and only lover had been quick, grabbing at her, in some sort of race to the finish line—and he'd always won. Leaving her dissatisfied and racked with remorse. She only knew quick. And that was how she wanted it now.

As Isaac's mouth left her neck and made its way through mind-melting kisses along her shoulder she reached down to his boxers and gave him a squeeze. He was so big. So hard. So...she closed her eyes at the thought of him inside her...damned scary.

He shifted slightly away.

Plucking up courage, she reached for him again. Squeezed. Looked up to see his reaction.

Which wasn't what she'd expected. He was looking at her again, as if she were some kind of child...his kid sister. The way he'd looked at her too many times—it wasn't a sexy *I want you* look. His hand covered hers and moved it away. 'Hey. Not so fast.' Then he whispered into her neck. 'Or so timid—it won't bite you. But wait. There's no rush.'

'I'm sorry...I thought...' Truth was, she didn't know what she thought. Or what she expected, past having him. But he had a different plan, she could tell. And she'd stuffed up. 'Was I doing it wrong?'

'No.' His eyebrows knotted as he gave her a gentle confused smile. 'But each guy has his own way.'

Obviously not her way. Either that or he was using code for *forget it, baby.* She twisted away from him, put air between them and as she did so she could see the sexual mist clearing from his eyes. He was starting to realise what a ridiculous idea this was. She just knew it. 'You didn't like it?'

'Of course I liked it. I just wasn't expecting it. Not so quickly. People tend to do a little getting to know each other first.'

'Great. I told you I was no good at this.' Suddenly feeling cold and exposed, Poppy stood and buttoned up her top. She'd rushed things and he wasn't ready. Probably wouldn't ever be ready. Was probably kissing her out of pity. Again. After all, she'd made the move, not him. Again. Her cheeks blazed. 'Oh, God, I feel so stupid. I should go. So should you.'

'Hey.' He caught her wrist, one hand reaching out and cupping her face, thumb running along her lip, making her shiver and yet hot again in so many places. 'Poppy, really? You want to leave without sorting this out? You think I can get to sleep now? Can you? After that?'

'I...I don't know.' But she gripped his arm and couldn't let go. Didn't want to let go. A rush of long-dormant hormones threatened to engulf her, definitely made her sway. Just looking at him made her heart jump and jitter and made little flashes in her belly like the twinkling Christmas tree lights. She hauled in breath after breath. This was ridiculous. She'd never felt like this. Out of control. But so turned on. Crazy.

And stupid.

Naive.

Embarrassed.

He pulled her to sit next to him back on the couch, dragged a thick mohair throw over them. Then he ran his hand down the back of her head, snagged into the knots from her fitful sleep. Gave her another of his gentle smiles. 'Now, what's going on in that head of yours?'

'I...I don't know.' A grown woman with a medical degree and that was the best she could do? She needed to try harder. Be honest. Because she did not want to have any kind of anything with a man without wide-open honesty.

That much she was sure about. Hell, she'd just about ripped off what clothes he had on—what could be more embarrassing than that? 'I want to sleep with you.'

'I kind of worked that out.' His smile slipped. 'There were a lot of clues. Nice clues. Very nice. But do I get a say in this?'

'Obviously.'

He tipped his chin upwards. 'Good to know.'

'I know you want me, too.' She looked at his groin, which didn't appear to be quite as hard or as big as a couple of moments ago.

His smile recovered. 'Yes. Yes, I do. That is pretty obvious. And no…I don't.'

'You think it would be a mistake.'

'I think it would be rash. And probably high up in the top sexual rankings of my life.' His fingers combed through her hair, tucking a piece behind her ear. 'You are beautiful and gorgeous and very sexy and very, very desirable. But…I'm not the guy for you. Seriously.'

She wasn't going to beg. 'And clearly I'm not the girl for you.'

'You know what I'm like, you said it yourself—one month is all I can manage—and that's the best I can do. That's not what you need.'

'And you know what I need, do you?'

'Where has all this come from? Why me? Why now? The other night you didn't want to.'

'I did. I was just trying not to. I want to learn about sex.' And, God, if that didn't make her sound pathetic.

He ran a hand over his jaw, one eyebrow raised. 'You want to use me for sex? Interesting.'

'It's not using you, per se. I'd hope you'd have some fun, too. I just want to learn. Stuff. For…later. When I'm back in the dating game seriously. When I'm at work and women ask me things about orgasms during penetration, or games to jazz up their sex lives…I never know what to say.'

'You've never had one?'

'An orgasm? No, not from a man. Not from Tony.'

Isaac's jaw tensed at the name. 'Why does that not surprise me? Did he ever give you anything other than abuse, stress and a lifetime of anxiety?'

Shame. Guilt. She had a list—a long one. 'I guess not.'

'But you must have…had an orgasm from…yourself? Surely? Otherwise it's been a long, long eight years.'

'Of course. I'm a grown sentient woman, Isaac. I have needs. How the hell do you think I've survived the past few years listening through flimsy walls to the comings and goings of my flatmates? Or watching sensuous films?' Geez, and now she was talking about masturbating, with Isaac.

'Ear plugs?'

'Really?' She threw him a frown. 'I get the feelings. I just haven't acted on them…much, at least not with someone else.' And now? Well, now she was almost overwhelmed by them. By him.

There was a subtlety to him—strong and yet gentle. Aloof and yet within reach. Funny and yet serious. Once again she was half-naked with him, in a makeshift bed, his bare shoulders sticking out of the throw. He had a small tattoo in the shape of a Celtic knot on the back of his left arm. A crescent-shaped scar, well healed, just below his shoulder blade. She'd known him almost her whole life and yet never really known him at all. The fine hairs on his arms glistened in the half-light, veins standing out along capable hands. Hands that had instilled intense pleasure. How could something so masculine give such wild sensations? How could that mouth make her wet by its touch? Those were the kind of things she needed to know—the small-print finer details of seduction—what turned a woman on. What did it for a guy.

'What's it like for a man? Can you remove emotion from sex?'

'Me personally? Sure. But only when there's a tacit agreement, otherwise it wouldn't be right. Or...' he searched for the right word '...honourable.'

'I'm not looking for honourable. I want to know what sex can be like. In the one and only relationship I've ever had I was vulnerable and trusting and I was hurt badly.' But he knew all this already. 'I want to enter my next proper relationship equipped with knowledge and skills. I want to know how to behave sexually. I want to feel in control of myself and my desires. I want to be independent. And having little sexual knowledge puts me at a disadvantage. I do not want that.' She shuddered at the memories. 'I don't want to ever be vulnerable again.'

'No. No, you don't. And I can understand you want to arm yourself because that way you can also protect yourself, too. Be in control. But what about afterwards? If I, or another lucky, helpful guy, did agree to sleep with you, then what? You know I can't give you what Lara, or Izzy or Tori have. You deserve better. Hell, you want better, Poppy, don't you?'

'What I'm talking about is exactly the kind of deal you strike with every woman you meet. Short and hot and limited to purely physical. That's all I want from you. No commitment. Because, believe me, I do not want to get involved with you—I'm not so stupid as to think you're a viable option for the long term. Call it a booty call. Friends with benefits.'

'We're friends now?'

She shrugged, aghast at the intensity of desire rushing through her. She couldn't do this with anyone else. It had to be him. If only to stop this physical need. 'Enemies with benefits, then. For a limited time only.'

Again with the hair stroking. 'Poppy, this is torture. It's a dangerous game you want to play. You say you won't care when we stop but you will. I've already seen you get your heart broken once. I'm not going to watch it happen again.'

'Oh, and what makes you think I'd fall for you?'

'How could you not?' He laughed. But then his face grew serious. 'I know you too well. I saw how that sleaze-ball used you. Lied to you. Broke you.' The anger in Isaac's face, in the shadows and lines, was almost as fresh now as it had been years ago. It had scared her then, but she'd been pretty sure he was only concerned that he'd wasted an evening of his precious time. Or was there something else? Some flicker of caring that he didn't want to own up to? She didn't want to think about that, so focused instead on his voice. 'But how would I be any better than him? Using you for sex?'

'You're exactly the man to choose... You know me better than anyone. I know you don't want anything extra. Last time it was all emotion and very bad sex. This time I'd know the score. It would be honest.' With a scathing look of self-loathing she pointed to her heart. 'You think I want to be like this? To be a successful doctor and yet a failure in the most important part of my life?'

'You are perfect as you are. As I said before, any man would be lucky to have you.' But it wouldn't be him, that was clear. He started to pull the throw down. 'But right now, it's time for bed. To sleep. It's late and neither of us are thinking rationally.'

She reached for his wrist, anger mounting—not at his rejection, but at his perception of her that didn't seem to have changed since that stupid day at the school ball. 'Okay, but it's your loss, Isaac. I'm not the same girl as I was then. I'm strong and capable. I'm not going to break into tiny pieces over you. I can survive. I'm a career woman who has poured her heart and soul into saving lives. I see people scraped off the streets and put them back together again. Gunshot wounds. Stabbings. I can deal with drug abusers and alcoholics. I help women give birth, share their joy and, if the worse happens, their sorrows, too. And then I get up and do it again the next day.'

At his open-mouthed reaction she rallied again. 'But you're right, you're not the man for me. The man I need is someone who has the guts to help out a friend. The ability to let go and have some fun. And who can see me for what I am and not for who I was a zillion years ago.'

She bundled herself out of the throw and stood up. 'Goodnight. And don't trouble yourself about getting rid of the mouse. I'll deal with it myself.'

Somehow.

CHAPTER EIGHT

'HEY, HOMEBOY, HAVE YOU seen the email I forwarded to you?' Isaac's right-hand man, Jamie, sauntered into Red with the widest grin he'd had since before he gashed his hand wide open. The white sling contrasted wildly with Jamie's black shirt. 'Another great review for Blue. Oi, cheer up, mate. That's what I call good news. The punters will be flocking in. Edgy, they called it, but with a... cosmopolitan flavour that appeals to the...after-dinner crowd looking for great dance music and a good vibe.'

Isaac forced a grin. Lifted down two beer glasses and poured himself and Jamie a drink. 'Here you go. A celebratory toast. That's great.'

And it was. Everything in Isaac's life was pretty damned epic compared to the dismal picture he'd had growing up. He had a string of successful bars, great mates and a not-too-shabby penthouse apartment, when it was finally finished. Which couldn't be soon enough.

Because, one week after the sex discussion and the atmosphere in the flat had cooled to the sub-zero temperatures of the Arctic Circle.

Trouble was, while his head had been busy debating the pros and cons of sticking his tongue in Poppy's mouth, his body had gone right ahead and done it. The only thing that had stopped him going further had been the look in her eyes as she'd grasped for his groin.

In fact the look on her face for the whole few minutes they'd been locked together had almost killed him. She was terrified. But, with a determination to overcome it, she'd rushed them into a situation neither had been able to handle. Then he'd made everything worse by trying to have a reasonable discussion. How to have a sensible conversation when both parties were turned on as hell?

But the second he'd clamped eyes on her confused and anxious gaze his heart had pinged. Pinged in a way that had happened only once before. And now he understood. Understood that the anger he'd felt for Poppy's first lover had been fuelled by something akin to jealousy. Unadulterated and righteous—hell, the man had been no more than scum—but angry jealousy nonetheless. Then, when she'd tried to seduce him a huge wedge of emotion had lodged under his ribcage. And he still couldn't shake it. Poppy instilled some kind of feeling in him that he did not want to contemplate. Or even acknowledge.

Which was why he'd had to put a stop to anything further happening. It wasn't that he thought of her as still a young girl—it was the opposite. He saw her now as an accomplished, professional, successful woman. Who was beautiful and honest—a little too forthright sometimes, definitely annoying. And who pushed his buttons in so many ways he didn't know what he was doing.

He swirled the last drops of his beer. 'Another?'

'Have you been listening to anything I've said?' Jamie frowned. 'Come on, Isaac. We're talking big bucks here. Focus, man.'

'Sorry. What was it?'

'Electrics. Bar Gris has been having problems with the electrics. They keep short-circuiting. It's a fire hazard. Marcel reckons he has it under control, but I don't think so, I think he's being fobbed off. One of us needs to go over and sort it out.'

Without hesitation Isaac knew he would be a better fit in Paris right now. And he'd get some space, which he needed. 'No worries. I'll grab a bag and get over there.'

'No. Actually, I was thinking you need some downtime. Real downtime. You've been covering for me for too long, zapping between Paris, Amsterdam and London. Why don't I go? You could have the weekend off.'

'And spend it where?' The last thing he needed was extra time in the flat with an angry Poppy. Or a trip home to his mother, which always ended up dysfunctional. And in both scenarios he'd have to spend uncomfortable time experiencing strange emotions swirling in his chest. Nah. 'I'm fine. I want to go to Paris. I like Paris.'

Jamie grimaced. 'Actually, I've already booked a flight. For me. And Steph. I thought I'd take her over for the weekend. You know how things have been between us. We need some couple time before the whole thing implodes. I've also spoken to Maisie and she's happy to take over the running of Blue this weekend—she is the long-term manager after all. We can't babysit her for ever. And this place almost runs itself. Why don't you take some time out and chill?'

'Because I don't need to. I'm fine. We have three bars to run here in London. We can't both take time out.'

'Yes, we can. Two nights, that's all. You've been working yourself ragged. Your head's not in the game at the moment. And the only reason I can think of is that you must be knackered. So go home. Sleep.' Jamie put his arm on Isaac's shoulder and turned him to face the front door. 'Hey, look, there's that girl that was in the other day. Friends of yours?'

'Izzy. And Harry.' Isaac gave a sharp intake of breath and glanced behind them at the swinging door. They were alone. 'Hi. How're you doing?'

'Goodness me, it's cold.' Izzy stamped her feet and

hugged up against Harry, who beamed. 'Oh, nice to see you here, Isaac.' She pulled off her gloves and threw them on the counter. 'Thought we'd have a quick snifter before we meet up with Poppy. We're going ice-skating. Any hot toddies going?'

'Sure. Two? Coming right up.' He poured two large steaming drinks and handed them over. That was the problem with having a bar so close to home—it gave people free rein to pop in unannounced. 'I don't suppose you're meeting Poppy here?'

'No. At the tube station. In ten minutes. She's still off the booze, apparently, so said she didn't want to come here.' Izzy bit her bottom lip. 'She's acting a bit weird. Don't suppose you've noticed anything different?'

What little time he'd spent in her company at the flat he'd noticed every nuance of her stiff shoulders, the aloof tip of her chin. The hesitancy and anger in her eyes. The simmering annoyance and undercurrent of repressed sexual attraction. Hell, he'd felt the same things, too. 'No. Nothing. But then we've hardly seen each other, to be honest.'

'Because he spends way too much time either here or at Blue,' Jamie butted in. 'He's starting to get on my nerves. Don't suppose you can whisk him away for a few hours? Days? Weeks? Maybe he'll come back refreshed and focused?'

And that was the first time anyone had ever accused him of not focusing on his work. He lived for his work. This thing with Poppy was getting to him. He had to speed up the renovations. Find a hotel if necessary.

Izzy clapped. 'Yes. Of course. Why not? Come ice-skating with us?'

'Absolutely not. I'd rather stick pins in my eyes.'

Harry laughed. 'Chicken. Afraid you're going to make a fool of yourself?'

Isaac interrupted the generalised chuckling at his expense, 'Hey, it's not that I can't—' *Much.* 'I just…' Saying he didn't want to would sound churlish; it was a nice offer. 'I'm busy here.'

'No, he's not. Take him. Please.' Jamie joined in. 'Find him a woman, while you're at it. He needs something… I think he's hormonal.'

Harry gave Izzy a fleeting knowledgeable rise of the eyebrows. 'Actually, to be honest you'd be doing us a favour. Poppy really wanted to go to see the Winter Wonderland in Hyde Park and we couldn't refuse her, seeing as it's her only chance of a break before Christmas…and everyone else is away. But, three's a crowd…you know?'

Izzy nudged him. 'Don't you dare say that. I love Poppy to pieces and I want to go ice-skating.' She paused, twiddling a beermat round and round. 'But four would be a good number.'

Yeah, right, if he tagged along as a crowd plumper Poppy would be just thrilled. Not.

Plus, he'd hate every minute.

Harry nodded. 'Hey, come on, mate. Don't let the women gang up on me, two against one. They'll have me making snow angels and looking at ice carvings. Queuing up to meet Santa.' He leaned forward. 'Solidarity, mate. Safety in numbers.'

'Nah. Sorry.'

Harry shrugged. 'Well, poor Poppy, I do hope she can skate. I mean, we'll try to look after her…but a man can only hold up one woman at an ice rink. I hope she doesn't hurt herself too badly.'

That was low, appealing to instincts Isaac hadn't even known he had until a few days ago. Having watched Jamie go through his romance with Steph, and Alex with all his conquests, Isaac had been wingman on too many occasions. So despite every misgiving he had he found himself agreeing, because he didn't want Poppy to be the spare part in what looked like a slightly skewed threesome. And after all the escalating tension in the flat some positive time outside might break the ice. Not literally, he hoped. 'Okay. Okay, I'll come.'

'Well, thank the good Lord for that.' Jamie smiled. 'Peace on earth and goodwill to all men is restored. Well, goodwill to me, anyway.'

'Great. Come on, then. Grab a coat.' Izzy downed her drink, took Harry's arm then paused, turning back to Isaac. 'Oh, did you ever find that mouse?'

And that was another thing. 'Yes. We caught it in the trap. Poppy took it out and set it free in Holland Park. I told her I'd do it, but she was gung-ho to do it herself.' Proving some kind of point. Which really wasn't the point at all.

'Poppy did? I thought she was terrified?'

'She was, apparently. But she wanted it gone and couldn't wait for me to do it. So she did it herself. Quite determined.' By the time he'd woken up the next morning she'd already gone without leaving him so much as a note. And why that had irritated him he didn't know. In fact, when he looked at it there were a hell of a lot of things going on in his head that he couldn't quite fathom. But they all seemed to start and end with Poppy.

Six loops around Hyde Park's temporary ice-skating rink hadn't anywhere near dampened down Poppy's irritation. She dug her heels in as she reached Isaac and covered him with a light peppering of snow. 'I thought you hated being cold.'

He blew into his hands but kept warm teasing eyes on her. 'It's warmer here than in the flat.'

'If you don't like the atmosphere you can always move out. No one's holding a gun to your head to make you stay.'

'No. But I figure if you think it's my life's work to annoy

you I'd better excel at it. At least, until Alex gets back, then he can take over.' He flashed a smile that did something strange to her stomach. Because, despite living the Cold War at home, she couldn't get the weird sensations out of her gut. Head. Lady bits. Although, in an attempt at an entente cordiale she had been at pains to remove her underwear from the radiator. What the heck was wrong with men that they objected to that, anyway? Plus she always tried to avert her eyes if he was dressed in anything less than his full winter overcoat. Which screamed sex, anyway.

She was doomed. And angry.

Bad enough to make a fool out of herself once. But twice? And now her so-called friends had insisted he join them. And then they'd sneaked away to a makeshift beer tavern somewhere on the edges of the rink, leaving her here with him. And the ever-present vibe.

They'd clearly been grateful for Isaac's presence, which meant they had plenty more time for each other. Heck, Izzy and Harry had been touch and go at one point in their relationship; they deserved some good times. Lots of them—particularly Harry, who was now shouldering an international business, and worrying about his father's ill health.

Those kinds of issues put hers into perspective—so she had a fatal attraction with a guy she lived with? It could be a lot worse. Couldn't it?

She looked up at the twinkling lights strewn from the centre pavilion across the rink. In the distance a large Ferris wheel turned slowly, lit up with white lights. It was beautiful, lighting up the dark cloudless sky. She needed to make the most of her three more days of freedom. It hadn't quite been the Zen chill-out that she'd hoped for. But she was going to enjoy this part, the magical Christmassy snowy part; Isaac could go to hell with his frown and his icy words and his...damned beautiful smile.

Sexy legs.

Capable hands, that made her tingle all over... She dragged her eyes away from him. 'Okay, I'm going to go round again.'

'Good. If you happen to pass a kiosk selling good moods, be sure to invest in one. Better still, I'll treat you to one. My shout.' He thrust his hand into his pocket for coins, wobbled, grasped the barrier as twenty or thirty laughing people wearing an assortment of bad-taste Christmas jumpers skated by. Managed to steady himself. 'You know what? I think I'll hang here.'

Pressing her lips together to stop the smile, she skated to him. 'You haven't done much skating?'

'I'm fine. Thanks. Don't worry about me.'

'What's the problem?'

'I don't have one. See?' He stuck his foot out and wobbled. Then the other one. Crashed to the floor. Looked up at her and laughed. 'Finally, a smile. Even if it is at my expense.'

'Well, the frown was caused by you, too. Idiot.'

'Hey. I'm the one hurting on the ice here.'

'Helpless idiot.' She offered her hand, but then withdrew it, preferring to see him struggle. How refreshing to not be the one making a fool of herself. For a change. 'Have you ever skated before?'

'Once. About a zillion years ago.' He pulled himself up by the barrier. 'I'm fine. Just finding my legs.'

She looked down the length of him. His leather jacket skimmed his trim waist. His legs were...perfect. The night sky was perfect. This wonderland of snow and ice, with its lights and laughter, was perfect and it suddenly seemed silly and unimportant to be cross with him any more. Her friends had skedaddled; she might as well make the most of the company she'd been forced to keep. And being better than him at something really gave her a kick. 'You want me to teach you?'

'No.'

'Come on.' She giggled. Actually giggled. Which was a surprise seeing as she hadn't giggled since last century. 'Hold my hand and I'll pull you along. You'll soon get the hang of it, I promise.'

He looked down at her hand and fitted his cold one into it. 'Okay. But be gentle with me.'

She tugged, but he tugged back. Hard. And she lost her footing, tumbling down with him, landing on the ice with a thick whump. Cold seeped through to her bottom. 'Double idiot.'

'Well, that brought you down to my level.'

'Oh, no, matey boy, there's a heck of a long way to go before I get that low.'

Propping himself up on one elbow, he trailed cool fingers lazily along her collarbone. 'And yet you want to sleep with me.'

She blinked. And shivered. And despite the cold she was definitely hot all over. 'Want*ed* to sleep with you. Past tense. I'm so over that. Missed the boat.'

'Oh, so you've changed your mind? Fickle, much?'

'Says the King of Fickledom.' She poked him in the stomach. 'Why are you here, anyway? I'd have thought this would be your worst nightmare.'

He shrugged. 'I needed time out from work. Fresh air... you know. All those late nights and clubbing isn't healthy... yada-yada.'

'Aka, they made you come. Because I can't think of one single thing about this that would tempt you.' And no, she wasn't looking for compliments. It wasn't as if she didn't see the guy every day—he could have offered an olive branch to her any time he wanted. He just hadn't taken the opportunity. In that same token, she could have, too—but anything past a brief hello had made her blood boil and her hormones escalate so she'd kept her distance. Something she couldn't do right now. She sat upright, looked for the barrier to pull herself up. 'Oh, God, don't tell me they were matchmaking or something equally draconian and embarrassing? Izzy has this desire to have all her friends as loved-up as she is.'

'No. Not at all.' He grabbed the barrier, levered himself upright, then offered his hand to her. 'Apparently I've been distracted. They thought I needed a break. But, I'm tired, is all.'

Taking his hand, she stood, brushed her jeans down, wiggling slightly to keep the wet patch away from her bottom. 'Don't you ever take time off?'

'Not if I can help it. I want my business to work.'

'To prove what exactly?'

'To prove nothing at all.' Although the way he said it made her think otherwise.

'So you ignore all your other…needs. And just work.'

'And that's a bad thing? Says Dr Workaholic, who ignored every need and…worked.'

'I didn't. I have a life.'

His forehead crinkled. 'Really? You have work, you mean. Your friends, meanwhile, have lives.'

'I… You… Damn.' No one had ever come out and laid that kind of blunt accusation at her. It was stark and raw and it hit her hard in the chest. Isaac was good at home truths. But then he, of all people, knew why she'd lived like that. Ignoring every need had been easy until now. Seemed she'd never really been tested. But she'd been running from pain and buried herself in her job—proving she was worth something. Proving that she was more than a stupid, infatuated teenager. *Home-wrecker*—the words made her stomach knot just at the thought of them.

Proving that she could achieve something for herself,

she'd buried the hurt deep inside her and used it as fuel. Was that the way Isaac had been, too? She'd known his home life had been rocky, that he'd almost disassociated himself from his family, but had things been so bad for him? 'I had my reasons for choosing to live the way I do. You know full well what they were. What are yours?'

And yes, she knew she was pressing hot buttons here, but there was more to Isaac than he ever cared to show and she wanted to scratch that fun-loving, too-handsome-to-be-true surface and see what was underneath.

'I like work.'

'Well, it's easier than dealing with deep stuff, isn't it? Family stuff? Stuff you'd rather not face.'

He looked away. Didn't speak.

She lowered her voice. 'You can tell me, you know. I guess it's about your mum?'

'Oh, for goodness' sake. There's nothing.' His eyes darted around to the crowds skating by, to the lights and the sky and the laughter. 'Like this is the right time and place, anyway.'

'Here's as good as anywhere.' She pinned him against the barrier. 'If you want to get away you have to bypass me.'

'What is this, an interrogation?'

'A concerned friend having a chat?' She couldn't help shaking her head. 'How about I give you a head start? Your mum left your dad for a younger man. She married. It didn't work, so she left. Found another guy. Then another?'

The frown deepened, along with a sadness in his eyes that made him look lost. 'Yeah, it's hard to keep up, right? Trading one in for another.'

'Then, she finally settled with a nice guy with a little kid. Then they had one between them. Boys.'

Pushing against her, he gave her a dark look. 'Are we done here? I'm getting cold. You look frozen.'

'And you look angry.' But as she processed what he'd said the penny finally dropped. *Trading one in for another.* Did he feel that his mother had done that with him? 'So you throw yourself into your work, growing your bars and business to feel worth something. To matter. To prove yourself.'

'You really do know how to push my buttons, don't you? Quit with the pop psychology.'

'Getting to the heart of things is my job. Besides, aren't we just two of a kind? Using work to compensate for other stuff.'

His gaze brightened as he looked at her. Her face, her mouth, back to her eyes—as if he was trying to understand something. Then he shook his head. 'I don't think so. We are very different, you and me. Because underneath that bravado you do want what your friends have, what Alex has with Lara. You want someone to love and to be loved and I don't get that. I'm fine on my own. I always have been. I'm fine.' And yet pain laced his voice. He held his hands across his body as a barrier, and he avoided eye contact when he spoke. He might not want to be loved, but he definitely didn't want to be hurt.

'One-month relationships are fine?'

'I've had no complaints so far.'

'That's because you never give them the chance to get to know you. Or to tell you what they want from you. Or to ask for more. Or to tell you you'd broken their hearts.' But she'd seen the odd one or two women, the tears as they'd left him. Or, more usually, he'd left them.

'And that's because I like it that way. And it's working fine. At least it was, until you decided to get drunk and then—*wham*, we're getting down with the touchy-feely stuff. It's not me. It's…well, let's say you definitely win hands down for irritating.' He pulled up the back of her jacket and pressed his cold hand against the small of her back.

'Says you? Get off me!' But a laugh bubbled up from her throat as he swiped his hand across her midriff to her stomach. 'Yeow. Get off.'

'Only if you shut up with the deep stuff.'

'It's hardly…probing…' He was too close. Too treacherous, too perfect. She got the feeling she'd agree to anything if he kept looking at her like that, especially when even though he'd refused to open up his body language had betrayed him, anyway. She scrambled away from him. 'Come on. Skate.'

'I'll give you one loop and unless you have me doing a triple-pike somersault or whatever it's called by the end of it I'll declare you a dud.'

'No duds allowed.' She pulled, tugging hard on his hand, but he didn't budge, his feet forming a tight V shape, toes pointing inwards. He was stuck. 'Come on.'

She skated back to him; he wobbled again, reaching for her. 'Whoa. Sorry. Legs still lost, I'm afraid.'

She wobbled, too, aimed to grasp his outstretched hand but grabbed his left thigh instead. At the top. Her voice thickened. 'No. Legs very definitely here.' And something else, too, very close to her fingertips. Her mouth dried and his name came out on a breath.

'Oh, God,' he gasped, his eyes fixing on hers, lowering to her mouth, back to her eyes. Something passed between them—something tacit. Suddenly her body was awash with awareness. Just to hear his unfettered need stoked the heat in her again.

The way he was looking at her made her think that the only way they'd ever get through this living-together thing was if they slept together, got it over and done with and stopped pretending or waiting for it to go away, because it wasn't going anywhere. He lowered his mouth towards hers. Stopped a few inches away. His breathing sped up, but his eyes…*God*, her heart thumped hard and crazy in her chest…his eyes told her what he wanted. What he needed.

But he was conflicted, too. Because he knew as well as she did that whatever happened next would draw a line under anything they'd done before. Neither was in any doubt as to what was at stake here—where this would lead. He knew what she wanted. She knew what he was prepared to give.

His misted, confused gaze bore down on her.

'Just do it,' she whispered. 'Forget everything else. Forget whatever it is that's stopping us having a little fun. I've been waiting so long to feel this. Just do it. I want you. You want me. Easy.'

'Hell, Poppy. You say that one more time and I won't be able to stop myself.'

She took his face in both hands. He'd rejected her twice—no way would she try a third time lucky. He had to want to do it. He had to make that move. 'Just do it.'

Then his mouth covered hers in a frenzy, a hard, fast, greedy kiss that instilled desire deeper, stronger, further inside her. He pushed her against the barrier, spiked her hair with his fingers. That hot, misted look still in his eyes, focused on only her. Questioning. Surprised. Concerned. And yet, so very, very sexy. 'God, Poppy, the things you make me want to do.'

'Do it, then. Do it all.'

'Just wait until I get you home.'

Her breath came in rasps, her head woozy with adrenalin. She couldn't feel, see, hear anything but him. 'Now? Should we go now?'

And even as she said it she regretted the push. Knew he didn't need to be rushed, knew there was no hurry. Unless, of course, she wanted to wring every last drop of him out before the end of the night, the week…*the month*. And there she was already making things complicated.

She so did not want complicated all over again. She wanted free and easy and fun.

'No, not yet.' But he pulled her close, wrapped strong arms round her as if committed to action. The future, no. Action, yes. But tonight was good enough for now. 'This is your night, your holiday. You can do anything you like here. Then I'll take you home.'

'You'd endure the cold and ice sculptures for me?'

He shuddered. 'Enjoy? I don't think so.'

'Endure.'

'Yup. That's the word. But if that's what you want? More of this place...' He tipped her chin up and took her mouth again, opening her coat and weaving his hand round her back, pulling her tight against him. Against his hardness and his heat. 'Or more of that?'

She could barely breathe for awareness. 'Why not all of it? Everything. And then, seeing as the flat's empty, we can do anything you want there, too.'

'Anything?' She felt his smile against her cheek. And then, just for a fleeting second the nerves returned. What if she wasn't enough? What if she couldn't do it? What if he was too much? What if it wasn't fun at all? Worse, what if she wanted more? 'Hmm, what about Izzy?'

His nose nuzzled in her hair. 'What? Does she want to sleep with me, too? I think Harry might—'

'Shut up. Of course she doesn't. What I meant was, it would be rude to just leave.' She started to undo her skates, the jittery sexy feeling mingling with anxiety. 'Any idea where she and Harry got to?'

'Not a clue. Still in the bar?'

'I'll text them.' But he came closer, sat on a seat and undid the laces on his skates, too. His body brushed against hers and there it was again...the buzz and the whirl in her stomach. Intense. Her phone beeped. 'They couldn't find us, so they've headed back to Harry's.'

'So, Winter Wonderland is your oyster. What do you want to do now?'

Apart from rip his clothes off? But yes, it was a little bit nippy to do that. She pulled a crumpled brochure from her jacket pocket. 'There's so much to do here. We need to pack it all into just this one night.' Work beckoned, and then she'd be too busy with Izzy's hen party and wedding in her downtime—or just too plain exhausted from work. 'We could visit the ice kingdom. Or the circus? Snow sculptures? Heck, let's do it all.'

He shook his head, his throat working. 'All of it?'

'All of it.'

His shoulders slumped a little. 'And then home?'

Home. This was actually happening. She shucked the nerves away. She was going to treat this as a fact-finding mission. She was going to do the sex without emotion. She was going to be the sex-savvy woman she wanted to be. 'If you're good.'

His slow, lazy smile transformed his face. 'And what do you mean by that? Bad good? Or good bad? Good good? Or, my current favourite, very, very bad?'

'Just good.' Then she slipped into step with him as they went to exchange their skates. She had no intention of making him do the rounds of the attractions. There was only one place she wanted to be with him, and it certainly wasn't outside. She just prayed that she could be good, but hoped, more, that she could be very bad indeed.

CHAPTER NINE

'ARE YOU SURE?' Isaac knew he needed to tread carefully. Poppy had put up a good show of enthusiasm—and God, she was hot. Too hot. So hot. But also so innocent. No, not innocent, because she certainly knew what a man wanted, how to turn a man on despite what she thought, but she was still...naive. So easy to be blasé outside, fully clothed. But now he had her in the flat, door closed. How they'd managed to get home without undressing each other he didn't know.

It was happening.

She stood in the centre of the lounge, her coat dropping from her shoulders into a thick woollen pool on the floor. Her smile was coquettish, but there was a nervousness to it. And hell, he didn't want to hurt her. But if she kept looking at him in that *I want you* way, well, he wouldn't ask again.

'Absolutely sure.' She nodded, slowly, keeping her dark heated gaze locked with his. Dark against light. Soft against hard. Pure against...well, he'd been round the block a few times. But never like this. Not with someone who stoked such a fevered response from him. He felt like she looked—a nervous teenager, the first time. And for a second he wavered.

'But, Poppy, you shouldn't learn these things from me, but from a man who...' Who what? The words stuck in his throat. A man who would love her, who would keep her safe, who could make promises and keep them. Not from someone who would walk away. Changed—yes, inevitably he'd change, he knew that much, but would walk, anyway.

She pulled her hair out of its tie, and let her curls fall loosely around her shoulders. Every man's fantasy. 'I said, absolutely, Isaac. Don't make me ask again.'

He took a few strands and ran them through his fingers, held them to his face. They smelled of citrus and her. His groin tightened again. Pure feral need ran through him. 'Any time you want me to stop, just say. Anything you don't—'

'I want everything, Isaac. Don't talk about it. Do it.' Her shaking fingers played with the buttons on her dark purple blouse. She flicked one open. Moved her hand lower—flicked the next, allowing glimpses of a pink lace bra underneath, creamy skin, perfect skin he ached to run his hands over. He was hard. So hard for her.

'Okay. So we're going to take this slow. Okay? No rushing.'

'Okay.' She swallowed, her throat working overtime. The little pulse at the base of her throat beat a ferocious tattoo. A frown settled across her forehead. Her fingers shook. 'Show me slow.'

And he almost gave up again. It was all kinds of wrong. Because he wanted to do it hard and fast. He wanted to be inside her. To take her. To make her his. And she could never be that.

But he could not imagine another second without kissing her again. Without feeling her skin against his. Her body against his. Her, around him.

When his mouth connected with hers any kind of hesitation evaporated. She tasted of everything he'd dreamt of. A zillion flavours of ice particles melting on his tongue. Magic. Wondrous.

As he kissed her his hands took over where hers had left

off. Undoing her bra made her moan, little throaty sounds that fired sensation after sensation through his body. He peeled the blouse from her and dropped it to the floor. Slid the bra straps down her shoulders and threw it somewhere. Who knew where? He didn't care. He stepped back a little and looked at her soft, perfect breasts, nipples pink and puckered. 'Oh, my God. You are so beautiful.'

'So are you.' Smiling, she reached for his T-shirt and pulled it over his head, her fingers lingering over his pecs. After a moment of just looking at him, eyes wide and bright, she kissed a hot trail across to his nipple and licked. Relentless need shimmered through him, white hot. Her arms circled his waist, hands exploring his back, his chest, his stomach. 'Oh, God, Isaac, why do you have to be so bloody magnificent?'

'And I thought you wanted me to teach you. You're doing just great as you are.' Pushing her hair back from her face, he cradled her cheeks and kissed her softly. Tried to be patient. Tried to show her slow, but the touch of her mouth set his veins on fire. He dragged his mouth to that pulse at her throat, slicked a kiss there, along her fine shoulder bone and down to her breast.

She arched her back as he sucked in a nipple, her eyes fluttering with pleasure as she relaxed and tensed at the same time. 'Oh, yes, that feels so good.'

'Then it's only fair I treat the other one the same.'

Her loud moan as he circled wet rings round those dark nipples spurred him further; she rocked against him and he wondered whether it would be he who pushed them to go too fast, who wouldn't last many moments longer. He ached to be in her, to feel her around him. To feel her complete him. This. This out-of-control fever that sent him perilously close to the edge.

With a swift move he unzipped her jeans, shucked them down her legs and left them on the floor, his gaze lingering over matching pink panties that skimmed her bottom as he picked her up and carried her to his room. 'Yours is too far. Stairs...' His breathing quickened—not with the exertion, but with anticipation of what was to come.

He laid her on his bed and straddled her, careful to hold his weight. Her hand went to his jeans' zip. 'Show me, Isaac. Show me how you like it. Tell me what you like. Tell me what turns you on.'

'Hey.' He touched her hand, regretting that by carrying her in here he'd broken the spell. 'You first. Then me.'

Dark sparkling eyes looked up at him. 'Why not together? Is that too difficult?'

'No. Not difficult at all—but I want you to relax and enjoy this.'

'Oh, I am. But we might as well do you, because I never—'

'"*Do you?*" What is this?' God knew why that street phrase bothered him. It wasn't as if this were meant to be more than sex. Emotion-free. That was what he'd told her he could do. That was what he always did. He didn't want to think further than that—didn't want to complicate something with thoughts and shoulds and maybes. 'Whatever happens we are both going to enjoy this. I have ways...'

Poppy saw the gentle teasing glint in his eye but it didn't help the new flush of nerves racing through her, mixing with the heat and the desire and making her thoughts jumbled. She'd never had a say in who got what before—and she'd always lost out. But that was too many years ago and this was now. She was about to have sex with Isaac Blair. *Good God.*

Relax? No chance. Wasn't it meant to flow better than this? Wasn't it meant to just happen without talking? 'I don't even know how to relax into this... Can we just concentrate on you?'

'Then that wouldn't be fair, would it?' He knelt up and shifted so he lay on his side facing her, propping himself up on an elbow. 'Are you feeling okay?'

'Physically fine. I think.' The bravado had well and truly evaporated. But she couldn't go on like this for the rest of her life, avoiding intimate contact. What the hell Isaac thought of her now she didn't know. But just a little respite, some space from the sensations that were threatening to overwhelm her, was helpful. 'Scared. A bit. To be honest.'

He gave her a small reassuring smile. 'Of what?'

'Of it all. Losing myself. Control. Doing something stupid. What if you're too big? If I can't do it? Everything.' It was too intense. All this focusing on her. Too real. Too much. She'd never had this—it had always been about Tony. Never about her. Sure, he'd pummelled her breasts a bit as he'd stabbed inside her. Quick. Hard. Hurt.

Isaac's voice brought her back to here. Now. His bed. His heat. His arms. His touch. He stroked her hair, which soothed her. 'You'll be fine, Poppy. I'm not all that—'

'Oh, no...' She shook her head, remembering. Hell, she didn't have to try hard—the man's boxer shorts had been at the forefront of her mind for weeks. 'I saw. Those black boxer shorts do not lie.'

His grin was kind. 'Optical illusion.'

'But black's supposed to be slimming. Which means you're even bigger up close.'

'Women and men are made to fit together. It'll work. It's been working for millennia.' He flipped the waistband of his boxers. 'You want to take a peek? See for yourself?'

'Oh...' Heat ran the length of her, turning her insides into molten liquid. An ache settled across her abdomen and then lower. A nice ache. Delicious—desperate. Wanting. Never enough. Never satisfied. Like a pulse, waxing and waning. Yes. She wanted to see him. Hold him. Feel him. *Focus on him. Focus on him.* 'I suppose I could.'

She reached for his shorts, eased them down his thighs and he kicked them away to the floor. And *oh, my God*— her breath stalled in her chest—he was amazing. She wrapped tentative fingers around his girth. He was hot and very hard. And the softening of his eyes as she gripped him sent waves of something shooting through her. If she focused on him, not on her, she could get through this. She might even enjoy watching his pleasure. 'Show me what to do.'

He wrapped his hand around hers and she felt him shiver as he moved her hand up and down—not too hard. Not too soft. Not too fast. Not too slow. His face was a mask of concentration. She leant down and covered his mouth with hers. Tasting him—a new taste now, fresh, elemental, hot, wet kisses that quickly slipped to a hungry pace. She started to move her hand more quickly, heard him groan. Heard herself groan as she rocked against his thigh. She wanted to feel him in her. On her.

He turned a little, parted her legs and his fingers sank into her core. With a splintering of vision she let go of him and sucked in air. 'Oh. My God.'

She hadn't known it could feel like this. That a man could give her such a feeling. That fingers could make her crave more and more. Before she could stop herself she was tearing her fingers down his back and asking for more. For him. Inside her.

He rubbed his erection against her inner thigh. The intensity of sensation at her core doubled. She moved away. Moved back. Wanted more. Wanted less. She shifted her bottom a little. He was pressing against her opening.

And then. At the touch of him against her shards of light exploded through her. It was a raw physical sensation. Greed. Hunger. More. Not enough. Not enough. She shifted again, felt him press against her, heard him groan. 'Condom. Poppy. We need a condom.'

'Isaac. Come back.' *Isaac.*

Isaac.

Barely believable. But real. He reached for his jeans. Too slow. Slipped on a condom. Too slow. And then he was back. 'You're so wet, Poppy. You're an angel. A bloody Christmas angel.'

'Now. Please. I can't wait.' She felt a sharp stretch. Then a push. Harder. A searing pain that made her catch her breath.

He paused. Kissed her neck, took his weight as he stretched out above her and murmured against her throat, 'Are you okay?'

'God, yes.' It hurt like hell, but the pain was receding and in its place was an ache that would not be sated until he was fully in her.

Then a gentle thrust. And another. Pure physical joy rushed from her abdomen to her toes, to her head. She squeezed against him. Tried to match his rhythm, moving beneath him, trying for faster.

'Hey. Slow down. If you do that it's going to be over way too quickly.'

His hand squeezed in between them, fingers finding a place that exploded her thoughts into tiny pieces. He rubbed as he thrust until she didn't know which she wanted more. His fingers. Him inside her. His kisses. She just knew she didn't want any of it to end.

Didn't want this to stop. To lose him. To lose herself. 'I want more. Can we do more? Another position?'

He grinned. 'You want to play, now? Are you sure?'

'Why not?' She shifted a little underneath him, felt bereft when he pulled out of her and the connection between them broke. 'I know there's heaps more. I just haven't ever done any. Can we try some? One?'

'You seriously want to talk at a time like this?'

'Show me.'

'Anything for you.' His smile was sexy and kind as he sat up on the bed. 'Okay, face me and sit on my lap. This one is great for maxed-out pleasure.'

She did as she was told, legs wrapped around his back, and he entered her again; this time he was so close she felt his full body the length of hers, skin on skin. He held her so tenderly, the intimacy was intense. She couldn't help but look into his eyes, watch as the sexual mist came over him. Kissed him deep and hard. Then the kissing became more powerful...more intimate somehow as she kept staring into his eyes. She was making him feel like this. Making him hard.

And then he began to move more quickly, more urgently and he moaned her name. Just hearing that voice, that word, made her heart contract. She wanted this, but she wanted him more. Wanted him in her today and tomorrow. And... 'Isaac. This is...this is...'

'I know. I know. This is... *You* are amazing. Oh, God, Poppy...' he growled as his gaze locked on to hers again as he stroked her cheek. His beautiful, intense blue eyes telling her that he felt this, too—whatever it was—this wondrous, unique sensation.

Then she couldn't think of anything. Only that the pleasure, the sensation, must never end. She heard a moan— it wasn't him. It must have been her. Heard herself cry out, beg for more. Beg for him to never stop. Her hand reached for his and their fingers tangled over her core as she clenched around him. Rubbing. Moving. Faster. Deeper. His body slick against hers, where he began and she ended she didn't know.

He arched his back and cried out. And then her body shook as wave after wave of delicious trembling took her over the edge into perfect, perfect bliss.

* * *

'Wow. Just…wow. That was fun, the best ever. Not that I have much to compare it to.' Poppy's head lolled against Isaac's shoulder. 'Thank you.'

'My pleasure.' He didn't want to think about her previous sexual experiences; this was not the time to be angry or jealous, even though his fists involuntarily tightened. He consciously tried to relax. Plus, he didn't like to compare. But in reality he'd never known any sex come close to that. Had never felt so connected to anyone before. Ever. 'First time lucky, eh?'

'I just didn't know…didn't expect it to be so all-consuming.' Her smile was satisfied and awestruck. 'A tick for the big O. Now I know what all the fuss is about. I liked it.'

'Good. Yeah, me, too. It is meant to be enjoyable.' But he wasn't so sure about the feelings rattling through him now. They weren't particularly enjoyable; they were…a mess. He watched as she came down from the high, the flutter of her eyelids as she finally let out a long, heavy sigh and curled into him. And he curled back into her, glancing out of the window, his curtains still open from the daytime. Outside, soft snowflakes swirled and fell silently. By morning London would be cosseted again by a pure white blanket. It was as if magic were being created by stealth—creeping slowly in, unnoticed—but tomorrow things would be changed.

He was aware, too, of the softening in his heart. The way he'd been unable to tear his gaze away from hers. How turned on he'd been to watch her come, to feel her around him—to smell her, touch her. How that naivety and wonder had chinked a piece of his heart. How *she* had chinked a piece.

Wow indeed.

Because that had never happened before.

And he sure as hell didn't know what to do about it.

But now, now that he'd taken the one thing she'd kept only for herself for the past eight years—her body, her sensuality, and a huge serving of trust that he'd treat it carefully—what the hell could he give her back?

Not what she needed. Not what she wanted or deserved.

Her curls grazed his nose as she snuggled deeper across his chest. She fitted just perfectly in the crook of his arm, long, lithe limbs entwined with his. Her heartbeat raged against his ribcage. He was still inside her. Didn't want to withdraw. Didn't want to let go. Didn't want to end this. But it was the only right thing to do—because if he didn't she'd get too involved. No one could do what they just had and not feel something.

Too much something. It felt weird, foreign. Comfortable and uncomfortable. Threatening the status quo that he'd worked so hard to establish. Man, he was okay on his own. He liked it. He didn't have to answer to anyone. Didn't have to care.

And he was starting to do just that with Poppy. Cared whether he hurt her. Cared who she had slept with—and what that had done to her. Cared. Period.

So he needed to get the hell out. Trouble was, it was his room. Their apartment. How could he leave?

Hell, he'd done it many times before—he didn't need geography to forge a distance.

He wriggled backwards, withdrawing, watching her sharp intake of breath as she curled her legs up. 'Sorry. Sore?'

She winced. 'Yes. But in a good way. Don't worry, I think I'll be ready again soon.'

'Whoa. Steady.' He smoothed her hair down because he needed to touch her, to keep some contact with her despite what he was going to say. 'Look, I think we need—'

'A moment? Yes. Just one moment. To catch our breath.'

Her smile was wicked and made him hard at the thought of her being ready for him again. Wanting him again. But it would hurt to do it again so soon. He didn't want to hurt her.

He'd thought he could do this. There was so much he could teach her: how to touch him, what turned him on, how to touch herself. How to tease, how to take the lead. How to submit to pure pleasure. What to say. How to prolong the ecstasy. Games they could play. Toys they could use.

Could. But wouldn't. The enormity of the mistake they'd just made shook through him. He should have known: Poppy was different. And now he was different, too.

'No. Poppy—'

'Then you can show me a few more things…because I don't feel as if my education is anywhere near complete. First, I want to taste you…'

He didn't think she meant his mouth. A groan escaped his throat. He was fighting. Losing, but fighting. Was there no end to the feelings she instilled in him?

Before he could answer she kissed him again. Gentle at first, but when she slipped her tongue into his mouth and writhed against him he was gone. Again. Lost in the experience of her. His brain was working overtime trying to find all the reasons why they shouldn't do this, but his body knew exactly what he wanted.

Her.

CHAPTER TEN

POPPY WOKE FROM her exhaustion-induced half-sleep to a noise. Somewhere out in the lounge. A scuffle or a scratching.

The mouse trap?

'Isaac,' she whispered, trying to squint at the green display on his digital clock. Everywhere and everything ached. Not just muscles. Parts of her that hadn't been stretched or even touched in such a long time. Her lips were sore from his kisses. Her chin raw from his stubble. A delicious raw. A *want more* raw. Although walking might well be a problem tomorrow. She stifled a smile. She felt well and truly spent. A wicked, wild woman.

The clock came into focus. Four-thirty-eight. 'Isaac.'

'Again already? Do you never sleep?' Isaac's voice was thick and deep and husky; his hand slid across her stomach as he nuzzled against her head.

Sleep? She'd managed what? Thirty-odd minutes. 'I'm a doctor—I get by on many hours without sleep. Whole weekends with not one moment of shut-eye. Think you've got the stamina for that?'

He grinned, eyes still closed. 'Hmm.'

'Listen...did you hear that? A scratching or something. A noise, in the lounge.'

'Maybe little Mickey has come back?' His mouth was on her nipple now; her gut clenched as heat shimmered through her. Glorious heat. A glorious night of lovemaking, of discovery. Most noticeably, that Isaac was a very attentive and patient lover who gave more pleasure than he received.

She didn't want to leave him, but just like the last time she'd responded to the mousetrap noise she couldn't help satisfy her curiosity. Make sure the darned thing had been caught and wasn't making merry with her Christmas baubles...the couch...her food.

And, yes, she had to admit she had fallen just a little bit in love with her four-legged flatmate and had been quite sad to release him into Holland Park's long grass after all. 'Maybe he's homesick. Maybe he's scurried all this way back home. Shall we go see?'

'Sure. Tomorrow. Later.'

'Now. Come on.' Reluctantly dragging herself away from Isaac's lips, she pulled back the covers and tugged at his hand. The curtainless window shed fingers of moonlight over his beautiful body. And for a second she was pinned to the spot just looking at him. The broad shoulders that had held his weight as he'd entered her, the hair she'd spiked her fingers through. The delicious dip where his back curved into his backside, the soft downy hair just there where she'd kissed, before she'd turned him over and taken him full into her mouth.

And suddenly she wanted to do it again. And again. To crawl back in beside him and let him enter her, to place her fingers on herself and have him watch. To watch him draw slow strokes up his erection. Watch him lose control. There was so much she wanted to do with him. To him.

She had, what? Twenty-nine days left, according to his record—if not less. A brief affair. A holiday fling—the kind of thing her friends had done once upon a time, while she'd spurned any male advances. Not any longer.

But twenty-nine days meant twenty-nine nights, too.

Her stomach tightened at the thought.

She blew out a slow breath. She'd known what she was getting into. Known he wasn't offering her any more than sex. And it had seemed enough last night. An hour ago even. Now, however, she wasn't so sure. And it wasn't as if she could share this delicious secret with anyone, talk things over, or have a girly chat... Her friends would have a fit if they knew what she was doing. Isaac came with a pretty bad reputation that even she'd been previously happy to broadcast. He broke hearts. Period.

Tori and Izzy wouldn't stand by and let her get hers shattered—not the first time she dipped her toe.

First time that they knew about, anyway.

Her brother's reaction would be worse. His best friend and his nun-like sister—she could see the fallout now, and she definitely didn't want to get in between Isaac and Alex's friendship. Hers were hard fought for and very precious; she had no doubt the guys felt the same. This was something they'd have to keep very secret indeed.

There was the noise again. 'Come on, Isaac. Come and see if Mickey's back.'

'Okay. Okay. I'm clearly not going to get any peace until I do.' He stood, butt-naked, sleepily scratching his head, and again the sight of him stripped the air from her lungs.

'Wait. Clothes.' She handed him a pair of black sweat-pants from the back of a chair, ignoring his frown, trying to drag her eyes away from him. But failing, because he was an absolute joy to look at. 'Put these on. Much as I like to see you naked I'm not sure Mickey would cope. It might scar the poor thing for life.'

'Well, I'm sure he'd love seeing you naked as much as I do. But hell...I feel way too overdressed now.' He threw Poppy a dark grey T-shirt, which she put on; it skimmed her thighs. She tugged it down, inhaling his smell, suddenly feeling a little shy to be so casual and yet intimate with him out of bed—especially after everything they'd done.

Things had irrevocably changed between them—could never be the same. Especially once it ended. She'd be back to smiling politely at his plus-one dates. Wondering how it was for them in bed. Whether he'd given them the same attention, pleasure. And the jokey entente they'd shared would be gone for ever. Because how could it not? How could it find a new equilibrium after this?

He watched her and smiled. 'It looks a hell of a lot better on you than it does on me. I'll go first, just in case it's not a mouse.'

'Why? What else could it be?' Suddenly panicked, she clung to his bare chest.

He pressed a hard kiss on her mouth, his hands gripping her waist and dragging her to him. Teeth against teeth. Protective. Possessive. Reassuring. Feral.

He finally pulled away. 'I'm sure it's just a mouse. Let's get this over and done with, then we can catch some sleep before morning.' Fingers trailed along her bottom, squeezing a cheek. 'Or we could find something more interesting to do...'

'Here, take this.' She handed him the softball bat, grabbed his hand and followed him out of the bedroom. As they crept towards the lounge they heard a louder noise. Not a mouse at all. Whispered voices that sounded very human. At least one distinctly male.

Isaac's fist tightened around Poppy's; he pushed her behind him. 'Stay here.'

'Like hell I will.' She kept hold as he increased his pace.

'Hey. What the hell's going on?'

'Oh, my God. Oh, my God, Isaac. You made me jump.' The flick of a switch flooded the lounge with bright light, and in the middle of the room, suitcases at their feet, stood Tori and Matt. Suntanned, stupefied and staring. Tori's voice was incredulous as her eyes took in Isaac's naked torso, Poppy's scantily covered legs and the hand-holding that connected them. 'And...*Poppy*? Really?' Her voice rose an octave. 'Poppy?'

Busted. Isaac's gut tightened. This was not the plan. How the hell would they explain this?

And what did it matter? They had nothing to be guilty about. Just two people participating in advanced adult activities. Consenting. Fun. 'Hey, guys. Good trip?'

'Great.' Matt grinned. 'Sorry, are we interrupting?'

'Hi.' Poppy stepped out from behind Isaac's back, grabbed a cushion from the nearest chair and held it in front of the T-shirt that showed her legs off to their full glory. But her cheeks blazed and she barely made eye contact with her friends. 'Welcome home. We weren't expecting you until...er...' She frowned. 'When were you supposed to be coming home?'

'Last night, actually. I sent an email. As it was, we got delayed. Clearly you weren't expecting us—look at the place...' Tori wrestled some of the smile from her mouth and pointed to the debris left over from last night's pash session. Articles of clothing littered the floor, couch, and the bra had landed on the Christmas tree. 'Interesting choice of decoration. I thought we were being burgled and I'd caught you in the act.'

In one act, yes. Definitely not the act Tori was thinking about. Isaac dropped the bat onto the sofa. 'Likewise. I'll sort it out tomorrow. We got a little distracted...' He was not going to explain or apologise. 'So, if you don't mind we'll be going back to bed. See you in the morning.'

'Okay. No worries.' Matt gave a know-it-all, well-done-mate smile that Isaac wanted to wipe from his face.

But Tori glanced over to Poppy, her smile slipped and she didn't move.

Neither did Poppy.

Isaac looked at her and she looked back at him, her face still bright red and yet devoid of any discernible emotion. Her hand dropped away from his and he knew in that instant that she regretted it all. Maybe not the sex, but the fallout, the explaining. The reality. Knew she wouldn't be coming back to his bed. This exposition was too intense, the connection too fresh and fragile and new to sustain under the glare of others.

Because knowing the tight-knit friendship Poppy and Tori had there would be post-mortem ad infinitum and Poppy just wouldn't be able to explain what they'd got themselves into.

For that fact, neither could he.

Poppy shook her head minutely. 'I'll just have a quick word with Tori if you don't mind? I'll see you…er…later.'

'Poppy. It's okay.' He reached a hand to her waist and tried to pull her close. He didn't know what to say to make it better—it wasn't as if he were going to make any kind of declaration, or offer her a future. But it would be better for them all if they went back to bed and reconvened later. Preferably never. For once he was well out of his depth. Genial Isaac who always had the right drinks, the right answers, knew how to do the right thing, was stumped.

But she shrugged him off. 'So, Tori, how was South Africa? You look amazing, great tan. Shall I put the kettle on?'

And he should have been pleased she was letting him off the hook. And normally he would have been. Hell, he never thought twice about cooling things off when liaisons started to get uncomfortable. But…well, this thing with Poppy was beyond anything he'd ever known and he didn't know how to react. Except to take her lead and do what he usually did.

Walk away.

* * *

Poppy watched as Isaac slunk back to his room and then let out a deep rush of air from her lungs. She couldn't do the walk of shame and follow him. To do what? How could they sleep now? How could they do anything now? When Tori and Matt would hear. Would question—and she didn't have any answers. Not for them and certainly not for herself.

Tori kissed Matt goodnight and sent him to bed. 'Save a bit of space for me in that single bed, won't you? Oh, wait, Poppy did you ever get it fixed?'

Poppy grinned at the memory of an over-enthusiastic sex session between Tori and Matt that had resulted in a broken bed and the red-faced next-morning admission to their landlady. 'It was unfixable. But I bought a new one, so you owe me extra rent for that.'

Tori grinned back, eyes glinting. 'It was worth it. Every penny.' Then she turned to Matt. 'Tomorrow we'll go flat-hunting, hon. Finally.' She put a hand out to her friend, eyes wide, whispering, 'To be honest I could sleep anywhere, that flight was so long. But you! Whoa. That was a surprise. What the hell is going on?'

'No, you first. Flat-hunting?' There went another friend flying the coop. She was going to suffer a bad case of empty-nest syndrome very soon when there'd only be her and Isaac left. *Oh, God*—how would that pan out? He'd have to go. That was all. Then she'd find herself a whole new set of flatmates.

Now that didn't appeal at all. She'd loved having this place with her friends around her. Loved her girly chats, her best friends who'd seen her through thick and—if only she'd been honest with them at the start—almost the very thin.

It was the end of an era.

No, she couldn't think like that. They'd still be friends,

just with extras, too—husbands, fiancés, maybe even kids some day. The group was just getting bigger, was all. It was still a group. Still her group. 'Tell me more. Tell me everything.'

'Oh, no. You can very definitely go first, Pops.' Tori pulled her through to the kitchen and closed the door, switched on the kettle and found two cups. 'You're sleeping with Isaac? Really? What's happening? Because this is so far from the Poppy I know, I'm very confused.'

You and me both. She felt so exposed. Not least because she hadn't a clue what was happening.

Desperately trying to keep out of the unwanted spotlight, Poppy shrugged as embarrassment shuddered through her. Not unlike the first time she'd been with a man. *Just a quickie before we go home? Atta girl. You know I'd choose you if I could but she needs me.* No—then she'd felt guilt and shame. Used. Dirty.

With Isaac she'd felt none of that. Just wanted, and close. Touching someone after being so independent for so long. So…lonely. Someone stroking her skin. Someone wanting to make her happy. She bit her lips together as unbidden emotions ran through her. She wanted it again. She wanted more. To feel normal, to give in to feelings and needs she'd locked away in disgust and refused to open for too long.

The embarrassment was just a reaction to being caught out.

Would it ever be normal for her? Would she ever feel happy about having sex?

She had. Ten minutes ago she had. She'd felt reborn. Alive. Vibrant.

Her jaw tightened. *Damn.* It was all so temporary. This feeling of absolute satisfaction was temporary. Isaac was temporary.

She hoped to goodness the embarrassment would be temporary, too, and not likely to last almost a decade.

Tori patted her arm. 'Pops, are you okay?'

'Oh, sorry. I'm fine. It was just tonight. I mean…we've been skirting around each other for a few days now, weeks even…'

'Try years? It was bloody obvious to all of us, but neither of you seemed to realise… Can't count the number of times we'd thought you would…you know. It was just a matter of time.'

'Really, you all thought—?' That this thing had been there all along? How come neither of them had ever noticed? How come no one had ever said anything? Had they? She'd been so determined to deny any vestige of sexual attraction to anyone she'd shut them all up with a stare. 'Things came to fruition a few hours ago.'

'Details, sweetie. Now. Everything.' Teabags were plopped into mugs. Milk taken out of the fridge. A packet of chocolate digestives opened and thrown onto a plate.

Her appetite had fled along with her dignity when she'd been caught wearing nothing but Isaac's shirt, and suddenly Poppy felt depleted, bone tired. Exhausted. 'I'm not going to tell you anything past we slept together.' *And it was epic.*

'But, Poppy. You don't sleep with anyone. Ever. Not in all the time I've known you. So why choose Isaac? Why now?'

Poppy shrugged. 'It was an itch and we needed to scratch it.'

Tori threw her an incredulous look that said, *as if.* 'So what's going to happen next? Are you two dating?'

'No.' Slumping down at the table, Poppy forced a quarter of a biscuit into her mouth. Crunched. Chewed. Swallowed, with little enthusiasm. 'Relationship status—complicated. Or very simple—there isn't one.'

'Do you want one?'

'It's not an option for either of us. We're both too busy, too—'

'You could make time.' Tori came over and put her hand on Poppy's arm. 'Or is it another one of Isaac's crazy ideas? Friends with benefits? Does he just want cheaper rent? Because I'd have slept with you, too, if you'd dropped it by fifty quid...' She winked just in the nick of time. 'Joke.'

'Yeah. Hilarious. No, we haven't discussed anything, really. It just happened.' They hadn't needed to go beyond *just do it*.

Tori poured hot water into their mugs, smiling gently through the steam. 'But you know what Isaac's like. He's never here, for a start. He's hardly a contender for husband of the year.'

'I don't want a husband.' And, yes, she knew all this already. Tori's reality check wasn't helping to put things into perspective.

'You didn't want sex, either, Poppy. For how many years? Which brings me back to my original question. Why now? Why him? I mean. He's gorgeous. But—' In response to Poppy's anxious face Tori threw her arms round her friend's neck and gave her a hug. 'Okay. No more questions. I don't want to push you into a corner. Just be careful. You have a sensitive heart, Poppy Spencer, and I don't want to see you get hurt. Hurting's what he does.'

'I know. I know exactly what he's like. And that's why I'm not going to let myself get involved.' Which was the first big fat lie she'd told Tori in quite a long time. Because she had a feeling that it was already too late. Sex without emotion hadn't happened. Emotion had been there between them, deep and fierce and raw, and neither of them could deny it.

Just thinking about the way he'd looked at her had a thick lump forming in her throat. The way he'd made her feel. And that made things even more complicated because he was bound to run a mile now. 'No one else knows about this. You must promise not to tell any of the others. I can't face any questions, not when we don't know what's happening ourselves. And swear Matt to secrecy, too.'

'I will, I will. But promise me you'll protect yourself. And I'm not just talking condoms. I'm here if you need me, Poppy, any time. For a chat. Anything. I'm still shocked. I've never known you to have sex before. You look different. In fact, it suits you.'

She leaned close and squinched her eyes, peering at Poppy's face. 'Okay...one teeny question...just one.' She lowered her voice. 'Was it good? Come on. This is Isaac we're talking about. *Isaac.* Of all the men we know you have to go and choose the best-looking—Matt excepted, of course—most edgy and streetwise of them all. He's like...the full Monty with a cherry on top!'

'It was bloody fabulous. Okay?' Poppy resisted a fist-pump. 'Now stop with the questions.'

Tori leaned back, took a bite of biscuit and frowned. 'Seriously, if he hurts you, I'll break his legs.'

'Thanks, but if he hurts me, I'll do the leg breaking. And I'll break anything else hanging below his waist. I'm a doctor, I know how to do these things.'

'Well, then you can teach me.'

'You won't ever need it with Matt. He's just perfect for you.'

'Just shows you what a good judge of character I am.' Which was a hell of a joke considering the loser boyfriends Tori had brought home in the past. The list started with cross-dressers and got a whole lot worse from there. She'd eventually, with the help of her friends, discovered that relationships were all about giving and not receiving. In other words, Tori had grown up.

'Finally you are, yes, after a few false starts and dodgy

partners. Matt is lovely.' For the first time in a while Poppy laughed. Thank God for her friends. 'I know it's beyond cruel and we always share everything, but truth is, I don't know where this thing with Isaac is going, if anywhere. Which I doubt. So I'm not saying any more, it's late and I'm tired.' And, like Tori, in shock. And still a little embarrassed.

But not regretful. She was proud that she'd followed through on taking what she wanted. Felt powerful that she'd taken Isaac again and again, that she could make him want her, too. And she'd already added a little of the *Kama Sutra* to her sexual repertoire. That had to count for something? 'But I do want to hear all about your trip.'

Tori's eyes widened. 'Oh, well…I was going to wait, rather, we were going to wait and announce it, but…I have to tell someone or I'll burst.'

'Announce what?' Poppy's heart sped up a little. Good news clearly, judging by her friend's ecstatic grin. Tori had already let the cat out of the bag about flat-hunting— so things were still very serious between the two of them.

Tori handed her tea mug over but when Poppy took it her friend kept her hand out and waved the fingers of her left hand. 'We have news…'

A stunning solitaire diamond set on a white-gold band sat on her ring finger. Poppy jumped up and hugged her gorgeous friend, the lump in her throat surprisingly raw. 'Oh, my God. You got engaged. I hadn't noticed, I'm so sorry. How could I have missed that? It's beautiful.'

'You are a little distracted…I don't blame you.'

'Bad friend. Very bad friend. That's amazing. Just amazing. I'm so happy for you. Tell me what happened.'

Tori eyed her suspiciously. 'But I thought you were tired?'

'Not for this. This is spectacular news.' Her heart swelled at the thought of another wedding, another happy couple amongst her friends. And Matt was just the perfect laid-back foil to Tori's go-get-'em personality. If ever there were opposites that attracted and worked this was a shining example. 'Details. Now. Did he propose? I thought you were going to take things slow?'

Tori's grin spread. 'Well…you know I don't like to waste time?'

'Yes?'

'I asked him! It just came out one day when we were walking along the beach. Everything was perfect. He was, is, perfect and I don't ever want it to end. So…ta-da! He said yes and we're getting married. I'm a little shocked actually—it happened pretty fast even by my standards.' She beamed and Poppy felt a rush of love for her friend. 'But very happy.'

'You are one hell of a woman, Victoria. Does Matt realise what he's taking on?'

The love shone from her eyes. 'Oh, yes. And he says he loves me all the more for it.'

'I wish I had half your balls. Go you for taking what you want.'

It was so much easier to share her friend's elation than to delve any deeper into her own confused personal life. Everyone around her was loved up and settling down. And she felt as if she were in the slow lane swimming through thick soup to catch up.

No, of course it didn't matter that she wasn't engaged or planning a wedding. Of course she didn't really mind that her friends were starting fresh new lives. Without her. Away from the flat.

Their lives were changing, moving on. The past few years the apartment had been a cocoon of friendship, they'd simply carried on where boarding school had left off.

But change was happening, people pairing off, moving

forward. It was wonderful, the natural way of things and she was pleased to be able to share their joy.

But part of her, just a small part, wished she could have some of what they had.

And she knew it was never going to happen with Isaac. He was a stepping stone to being a fully-fledged independent and sexually aware woman, really. Someone she could hone her skills with until The One turned up—at least that was what she'd thought. Now she wasn't so sure. Emotion had become embroiled and she didn't know how to handle that.

So the next time she saw him she'd spell it out. Explain that this had been a mistake and that nothing like last night could happen again. And if that didn't throw a large ice-cold bucket of reality over their temporary liaison then she would treble the rent and hope like hell he didn't have enough cash to pay.

CHAPTER ELEVEN

ISAAC WAS NOT going to have it all thrown back in his face. He was not going to skulk around the apartment trying to avoid Poppy any longer. He would not spend the next few weeks being in the same space as her and not be able to look at her because things had got awkward again. Being at a wedding and unable to chat. Being in the damned kitchen and not able to share a cup of tea—or even talking to her alone without the Tori/Izzy chaperone she seemed to have amassed. Talking about anything other than what needed to be said. Leaving frosty notes. Back to texting one-word messages again.

Not being able to touch her.

His mind wandered back to the free way their bodies had meshed, uninhibited. No awkwardness there. He just couldn't get rid of the images of her, head thrown back, moaning as she'd folded around him. Or the images of her red-faced in front of Matt and Tori, guilty of nothing except enjoying herself. So he was damned well going to talk to her. Make sure she understood that there was nothing to be ashamed about. But that his life was chaotic and he would be shuttling from here to Amsterdam and Paris, that he could not be there for her geographically or in any other way she wanted. Or expected.

Trouble was, she was damned difficult to get on her own now she was back at work and things for his bars had upscaled to Crazy Christmas Busy so somehow a week had flown by in a stiff kind of silence and the tension in the flat had escalated to a surging boiling point.

And now he'd got back from the boxing club—once again disproving that exercise helped clear the head—and the flat was quiet. She could be in. Or out. But she wasn't making her whereabouts known.

After downing a pint of water he finally bumped into her outside the bathroom. She was wearing a full-length blue fleece dressing gown, hair scraped back in a scruffy ponytail. She looked sleepy. Sexy. Uncertain.

He stepped back indicating that she could use the bathroom first. 'You go.'

'No.' She glanced around at anywhere other than at him. 'You can go.'

A silence wove round them. Hesitant. Painful.

One of them would have to say something soon or it would get plain weird staring at the tiles, a huge cloud of anxiety hanging over them.

Go big or go home. Taking a deep breath, he started, 'Poppy, we need to have a chat. About things.'

Not a flicker of movement. She was perfectly still. Finally, she raised her chin and her dark eyes bore into him. 'No, we don't. We both know where we stand.'

'Do we?' He didn't have a clue. Which was a novel experience.

She nodded, curls bobbing around her shoulders. 'I'm good with it.'

'With what?'

'With what we did.'

'Oh? Because I thought you looked embarrassed.' Still did in fact. 'And there's nothing to be embarrassed about. It happened. These things do. We can move forward, be grown-up.'

She leaned against the doorframe, arms crossed over

her chest, attempting casual. Relaxed. Although the stance did nothing to hide the crackling strain in her eyes. Eyes that wandered over his body, his running top and shorts, stopping momentarily at places she'd kissed. Purred over. Licked.

Was this really a moment to feel turned on? He doubted it—but he did. Even at her most petulant she stoked a feverish kind of want in him.

She cleared her throat and her voice was all emergency-room professional *don't mess with me*. 'Well, thanks for the validation, Isaac, but it's unwarranted. I had sex because I wanted to. Nothing wrong with that. I can do it again, too, if I like.'

Now she was talking. 'Really? And will you?'

'I haven't decided yet.' Her eyebrows rose a little. 'Now, are you going to use the shower? Because I have a long list of things to do before the hen party this afternoon.'

He nodded. 'Oh, yes, the hen party at the spa? Then the hen-stag party at the bar?'

'Yes. The girls are meeting up first. Girly chats and all that. Massages…mani-pedis, man talk. You know the drill. Or maybe you don't, being a guy. Whatever. Then we're all coming round to Blue for drinks, apparently. Exciting.' She flashed a look that told him the prospect of spending the evening in his company was anything but.

And that was another thing. Joint hen and stag parties. Who the hell did that?

Poppy's lot did. Joined at the hip. Dating her would be like dating a posse. Handling the needs of one woman was bad enough, but four? He shuddered.

Still, hosting it at Blue meant he would be too busy working to be distracted by her. 'Be my guest—the shower's all yours. But if you're already going to a spa to be prettified what other kinds of things do you need to do?'

'Prepping…for this afternoon. We're only getting a

manicure and massage at the spa. There are other things a lady needs to do before she goes out.'

'Oh...so, you have to shave your legs and that kind of stuff...?'

'Why? It doesn't affect you.'

Yeah? Seemed everything she did affected him these days. 'Then maybe I should use the bathroom first. I've got to get to work and prepping takes a lot of time, in my experience.'

'Well, you should get a decent electric razor, then.' She eyed his legs. 'And do it more often. You've got terrible re-growth. Try threading? IPL? Waxing? If you need anyone to rip hot wax off your hairs I'll be first in line.'

Why the hell was she so angry with him? 'You'd enjoy that, wouldn't you?'

'Every second.' She opened the bathroom door and he got the distinct feeling that she wasn't angry so much as frustrated. She wanted something she couldn't have. But she'd decided she couldn't have it when she'd dropped his hand and refused to go back to bed with him. Her mouth tipped into a smile just short of evil. 'Actually, I've decided that I am going first and I'll be as quick as I can. But please don't use any taps until I'm done. The water supply's gone weird again. The plumbing really does need sorting.'

Now this was one thing he could do to make things a little easier in the flat. 'It might be the cold; freezing pipes are not happy pipes. Although, face it, they've been shot for years. I could get one of my guys to have a look if you like? Pretty reliable. I could talk to him about mates' rates?'

'Would you? I never seem to have the time. Although having just had more than a week off I should have put it higher up the list.' The tautness in her shoulders relaxed a little now they were talking about something that wasn't contentious. The smile turned warm. That almost cut him in two. It certainly warmed him in places that had been very warm a week ago. In bed with her.

'Well, you were pretty busy. Other things on your mind?'

Her eyes widened as her gaze locked on to his and the anxious, angry tension was replaced by a very different kind of tension altogether. The air around them super-charged, a crackle of electricity that rebounded between them. At the memory of tangled sheets the pulse at her throat quickened. She licked her lips. They had been dry. Now they were wet. He imagined wetting them more with his tongue.

Her mouth opened just a little bit—just enough. 'Yes. I was…distracted.'

'Very.' Heat fizzed around them, shimmering. He inched closer, unable…unwilling…to have another second without touching her. He thought she might move away but she didn't. She just kept on looking at him, eyes not moving from his. A dare almost. *Just do it.*

Then she stepped closer, too, her hand reaching for his shirt, fabric bunching in her fist. Her take-no-crap voice softened, eyes sparking a zillion wicked promises. So startling, the change in her. Breathtaking. She bit the bottom of her lip and smiled up at him. 'This is happening again, isn't it?'

'Yes. It is.' Ignoring the shadow of doubt that had put down roots in a corner of his mind, he stepped her into the bathroom, smiling against that pouty mouth that made him hard. He clicked the lock, not willing to chance any inter-ruptions or being caught, which would doubtless send her scuttling away again. 'Just once more for good luck.' Just to straighten things out between them, to smooth the waters.

He pulled her hair tie and let her curls fall over her shoulders. Stroked her cheek with his thumb, relishing her soft skin, the heated flush. 'But you see…here's the thing about showers…you don't want to use up too much water. Bad for global warming.'

'Is it?' she whispered.

'I don't know. It's bad for something.' He shrugged, far too concerned about current issues right here than global ones. His fingers trailed along her throat. 'How about we double up? Save the earth and all that.'

Thumb running along his upper lip. 'Oh, well, if it's for a good cause I can hardly refuse. We have to do our bit for the environment.'

He sucked her finger into his mouth. Watched the rapid flicker of eyelids that told him she wanted him. Very much. He grabbed her hand, nipped her forefinger. 'Excellent.' Her middle finger. 'Shower first. You are very dirty.'

'You, too. Very sweaty.'

Ring finger. 'Then we'll talk.' At her frown he backtracked a little. 'Or we'll talk first?'

'I have no intention of talking.'

'That's a first.'

Her eyes darted to the shower. 'And so is this.'

He twisted on the tap and a shot of icy water fizzed out. While he waited for it to heat up he took the opportunity to kiss her again, cupping her face, his lips pressed against hers. She tasted sweet and fresh and new. Exciting yet familiar. His heart thrummed hard in his chest.

Like coming home. Like Christmas come early.

She nipped his bottom lip with her teeth and he laughed, yelped. Unbuttoned her dressing gown and let it fall to the floor. The outline of two tight nipples pressing against her pyjama fabric made his mouth water. He gently stroked one watching her writhe under his touch. She pulled his face up to hers and gave him an urgent open-mouthed kiss filled with the past few days' need. Hungry. Wet.

Dragging her under the shower head, he leaned her against the wall. Water sluiced down his neck, over his arms, soaking his clothes and slicking them to his body. 'I do love these pyjamas. But I love them more when they're over there, and we're over here.'

He peeled her wet top from her body and threw it on to the bathroom floor. Then wiggled her bottoms down and kicked them to the side. He sucked a puckered pink nipple into his mouth, relishing her moans, the hand fisting into his hair. Gripping and pulling. He knew exactly what she liked, where she liked to be touched. What made her ready for him.

Everything felt light, electric. She felt perfect underneath his fingertips. Water dripped over the soft mounds of her breasts, running in rivulets down her cleavage. Heat surged through him, to hell with any doubt. He needed this.

Needed her.

He'd never needed anyone. Made damned sure of it his whole life.

Emotion plus sex.

Alarm bells began to ring in his ears, echoed in his heartbeat.

But he didn't care. Couldn't stop. He needed to be in her. With her.

She pulled at his top, dragged it over his head, laughing. 'I hate this T-shirt. And these shorts.' Her fingers made him groan as she shucked his jogging shorts off. 'But I do love these boxers. Oh. Not black today?'

'Red. Black. Whatever. Change is a good thing. Embrace it.'

'I fully intend to. I'm definitely embracing these.' Her hand slid along the front of his waistband, making him inhale sharply. She'd grown so much in confidence, knowing, in a very short space of time, exactly how to touch him to give maximum turn-on effect.

His voice was a growl against her neck. 'That prepping you have to do—how long does it take?'

She shook her head. 'What prepping? Did I not say I have hours to spare?'

'Me, too. How convenient. New housemates' rule. No clothes at all.'

'Okay. It's a deal.' She started to laugh as her hand cupped his backside and squeezed her against him. 'A few weeks ago I'd never have imagined me doing this. Naked with you?'

'It's amazing what you can do if you let yourself go.'

'I'm pretty gone. I have to admit.' She tiptoed her fingers around the top of his thigh. 'But I must warn you, this wet and wild experience is purely for research purposes.'

'How so?' He nipped her throat and pulled her under the water again.

'A client asked me about orgasms the other day—she wasn't getting any with just penetration—and I was able to make a few suggestions to help her.' Her smile widened and she gave him a dirty grin.

The bellow that came from his throat was quick and loud. 'Anything to help modern science. Come here.'

He squirted shampoo into his hands and slowly massaged it into her hair while she soaped his chest, his waist. Gasping when she took his erection in her hands and squeezed, sending shock waves through him.

But rinsing off the bubbles she pulled her hair tight back—making her look eighteen again and he was reminded of her innocent heart. How inexperienced she was underneath the bravado. No relationships over the years to harden her to the inevitable hurt of break-up. Even after a fling the rejection often stung. Apparently. That was what he'd heard—never being the one to be rejected. Something else he made sure of. He wouldn't ever give a woman the chance to cash him in for an upgrade.

'Are you sure about this?' Geez—he was the one with

the questions when he'd been assuming it would be her all along.

'Of course. But Tori says that if you hurt me she'll break your legs.'

Trying not to smile too much, he took both her hands in his, reluctantly drawing the delicious attention away from his hard-on. 'It's not my intention to hurt you.'

'You won't.'

'But I can't promise—'

Her finger covered his lips. 'I know and I'm not asking. So stop talking...I'm a big girl now and can look after myself.' Then she reached out of the cubicle to the bathroom cabinet. Fiddled around for a couple of seconds, and pulled out a small foil packet. 'See? Voilà.'

'Handy place to keep condoms.'

'Be prepared, I say. What kind of gynaecological registrar would I be if I didn't always practise safe sex?'

'Top of the class, Poppy Spencer.' He nuzzled against her neck. 'Vying to be teacher's pet?'

She froze. Pulled away. Her smile wavered at a memory. Fleeting. She shook her head and he realised what a dumb-ass faux pas he'd made. 'Pops. I'm sorry.'

Of all the stupid...

Why the hell had he brought that up? Now? For a moment she looked at him, God knew what the hell was going on in that head of hers. He thought she might hit him, jump out of the shower. Cry.

But she did none of those things. Instead, she took his hand and placed it on her breast, took the other one and squeezed it between her legs, pressing against her core. Rubbing slowly. Slowly. Placed hard kisses along his jawline. Bit him playfully and smiled. 'Just shut the hell up, Isaac. You are so not him. And look at me. Look at me.'

And so he did. He drank in her adamant pout, the honeyed eyes, the mussed-up hair. The perfect breasts that turned him on and the long legs he loved having wrapped around him. 'I'm looking.'

'And do you see that sad, pathetic, mixed-up kid?'

'Not at all.'

'Good. What do you see?'

'A beautiful, amazing, accomplished, naked woman.'

'Who wants you. And right now, if you please. There is nothing left of that girl. She's a memory. So kiss me again.'

God forgive him, but it was better to believe her—to go along with her—than to argue and blow this perfect scenario to smithereens. He'd probably go to hell and endure a thousand deaths but she was too much, too amazing to resist. 'Okay, if you insist. You're the boss.'

'That's the plan.' Not inviting any more discussion, she raised one of her legs and wrapped it around his hip. Taking her lead, he positioned her against the wall, and slid deep, deep inside her, his breath hitching at the tightness of her around him. The immediate intense rush of sensation almost knocked him sideways. He wanted to fill her again and again. And never stop. He gripped her, held her tight. Pressed rough kisses on her mouth.

In response to his primal impulse she kissed him back hard, urging him to thrust deeper. Faster. Fingernails dug into his shoulder as she braced against him, breasts pressed against his chest. Even with a condom he could feel her heat, her wetness as she squeezed around him, matching his rhythm in perfect time.

She gasped. Tensed a little. Then rocked against him. 'Oh, my God, Isaac. I've missed this. Missed you.'

So much for not talking. But it was cute. He cupped her cheek and pressed kisses over her face, while sliding in to the hilt. Deeper. 'What? Since last week?'

She gasped again, her words coming in short breaths. 'Since for ever.'

For ever?

Then she smiled, head thrown back as he filled her over and over—a perfect fit, a perfect match. His heart felt as if it were bursting into a zillion pieces, because she was right: despite every attempt to deny it—this had been growing between them for ever. Whatever it was, whatever was happening he couldn't name, but he knew she would be the only one who could put his heart together again. He thrust again, slowly this time because any faster and he'd lose himself.

But she pushed him to go harder. 'Oh, my God, Isaac. Don't stop.'

'Yes. *Yes.* Yes.' He could feel her tightening around him. Feel her growing climax as she increased the rhythm again, heard the moan that turned into a cry and that spurred his orgasm, shaking through him, blowing reality into a thousand glittering shards. He held on to her. Tight. Tighter, never wanting to let her go. Wanting this to last...yes, for ever.

As she rocked against him her head lolled forward on his shoulder and she nuzzled the soft spot at his neck in the last slow throes, her scent making his head swim. He turned his head and saw her eyes misted in a haze of spent desire, and she caught him looking, held his gaze. Moments passed and he couldn't find words to describe what this feeling was in his chest. A pressure building. But he realised that a new truth glittered between them now, a new connection...deeper and stronger than the last.

But even as they clung to each other that doubt he'd fisted down earlier sprang back with full force. He'd said he wouldn't hurt her, but it would happen in the end. He couldn't give her what she wanted and already she was in too deep—the look in her eyes told him that.

She was right: he couldn't remember a time when she hadn't been in his life somehow. Always there in the background. At first annoying, then entertaining. Then offhand. Then accommodating. Then…everything. But always there, with a ready if somewhat hesitant smile. He'd watched her grow up into a decent professional doctor. A good friend. A loyal sister. Fun. Serious. Sexy. Wow—that still felt new and weird.

He'd spent years wondering what a perfect woman would be like.

She'd been here all along.

And if he wanted her to stay in his life somehow—and he did, but back on the peripheries of his hard-fought-for, chaotic and commitment-free existence—if she could somehow remain untainted by this, then he had to put a stop to all this and let her go.

'Okey-dokey.' She sounded breezy and carefree as she levered herself away from him, switched off the still-running shower and grabbed a towel. 'I really do have to get ready. Is it okay if I finish off doing my stuff here?'

He found her a smile—it wasn't hard. 'So that's it? You've had your way and now *it's on your way*?'

'For now? I'm going to be awfully late if I don't get a wriggle on. I've got to dash. Thanks for the…research.' Her choice of words was very different from the stifled catch in her throat. She was trying to be light and stress-free, and failing. Something irrevocable had happened and they both knew it. 'I'll see you tonight? At Blue? Then maybe later…? I imagine Tori will be staying over with Matt so that means this place is available for us to activate our new no-clothes policy…' She pulled him to her and kissed him full on the mouth.

With just a simple touch of her lips he was hard for her again.

Damn. His hands were on her shoulders, creating just a little space. He needed about five thousand times more than he actually got. 'Look, stop. Enough. Can we just get something straightened out here?'

She paused, frowning, fist over a bright purple razor. 'Sure. What?'

He exhaled a heavy breath, saw the wince in her eyes as she steadied herself. 'Poppy, what do you want from me? From this? Because I don't do this. And you definitely don't. I'm hardly ever here, at some point soon I've got to go back to Europe—who knows for how long?—to get the bars sorted… You're busy at work…'

'Will you stop trying to analyse it to death? Let's just have some fun.' She held his gaze, her dark eyes swimming with undeniable affection, but he was drawn to them, to her, like a moth to a flame. And the thought of leaving again and going to stay in some cold, dingy hotel under a grey Parisian sky didn't appeal, not one bit. Which was mighty strange considering he loved Paris. That was where he had fun. In his bars, at work. Choosing venues, building his brand. *Working.* Not in the arms of a woman—at least not when his heart ached to stay. That never happened. He made sure of it.

So why the hell it was so difficult to distance his heart from his head this time he didn't know.

She tapped his backside with an open palm. 'Now, go and leave me to make myself beautiful. Go. Please. You do not want to watch me shave my legs.'

Then she ushered him out of the bathroom. Wet. Bedraggled. And still searching for the kind of words that would give him some semblance of peace.

CHAPTER TWELVE

'Why do spas always play this strange, tinkling, hippy ocean music? I feel like I'm in a birthing centre ready to deliver a whale or something.' Tori tightened the ties on her white bathrobe and sat down on a pure white sofa in the spa's relaxation lounge. With her deep tan and long blond hair Poppy thought she looked like something from an advert, gorgeously svelte as ever as she poured pink champagne into three flutes, engagement ring twinkling in the low-lit mahogany-walled room. Definitely not about to deliver a whale.

The gentle smell of lavender and ylang-ylang filled the air and seemed to be imprinted on the towels and plumped-up cushions, emanating good karma along with the chubby golden Buddhas grinning at everyone, hands on fat tummies from various corners of the room.

The outward calm contrasted with Poppy's inner excitement. Actually, it was more like excitement tinged with turmoil. All very well to play the detached, carefree card— but the problem was *feeling* it.

Anyhow, she refused to think about Isaac while she was celebrating her friend's upcoming wedding. She was going to live in the, hopefully, many moments of today's alcoholic hilarity. Then, tomorrow, after her body had absorbed the soothing aromatherapy vibes she would be fully Zen about Isaac and their…affair. Detached. That was what she was going to be. As soon as she'd worked out how to unattach her feelings from the very mention of his name. 'The plink-plink is supposed to enlighten your chakras. Or something.'

Izzy nodded. 'It does. But it just makes me want to go to sleep. Which is not what I need for my impending joint hen and stag night.'

Tori shook her head and laughed. '*Hag* night. Funny!'

Both Poppy and Izzy sat up. 'What?'

'Hen and stag. Hag.'

Izzy chuckled. 'Not exactly the image I was aiming for. I prefer stag and hen. Sten. Sounds kind of...German.'

Poppy picked up the tray of booze; no longer on the wagon, she intended to have some fun. 'Sten means "services" in Dutch. Services rendered? What do we have in store for us tonight?' She doubted much could beat the way her day had started. Sex in a shower. It had taken a lot of will power not to blurt that out in the steam room when the conversation had taken a decidedly devious tone. 'Take a glass each, ladies. Let's get this party started. We need to propose a toast.'

Poppy took hers and nestled into a soft, sumptuous chair opposite her two oldest friends. What a day. What a month. Her friends getting married, engaged, moving on.

And sex.

Sex with Isaac. *Blimey.* Her cheeks blazed at the memory. She cast a quick glance over to Tori. So far she'd stuck to her word and kept Poppy's dirty little secret, although she had given her plenty of strange concerned looks under raised questioning eyebrows.

'To darling Izzy. The first one to become an old married woman. Well done. Good luck. And...' She fought down a lump that had slipped into her throat. Nothing that a bit of champagne wouldn't dislodge. 'Never forget that we love you, you old...hag.'

'I love you all, too.' Izzy chinked. 'Thanks. Thanks so much, hags in waiting.'

'So good to see you glowing.' Poppy took a long drink. 'But a bit nauseating, really. All that happiness.'

Tori agreed. 'Sickening, actually.'

'Jealousy will get you everywhere. Besides, Tori, look at that diamond on your finger. Who'd have thought we'd both be almost old married women by the end of the year?'

Before she caught her friends looking at her with their usual sweet 'there, there, darling' puppy pity, Poppy suddenly found something very interesting in the hem of her robe.

She was happy for them. She was. Truly. Ecstatic.

Izzy downed the champagne and grinned. 'Cheers.'

'Hey! Hi! What have I missed? So sorry I'm late.' With a blast of cool air from the main reception area, in swept a flushed and breathless Lara, looking oddly out of place dressed in a thick coat and winter boots when everyone else was naked under their fluffy robes. But Poppy was grateful her arrival had changed the emphasis of the conversation away from happy and settled coupledom, all bright and rosy long term, when she'd had a bright and rosy start to the day but had no bloody idea how it would end—with Isaac or not.

She pulled herself up by her fluffy robe straps. 'Lara! You made it!'

After the group hugs Lara grinned. 'Sorry. Our flights were rerouted because of the snow. I thought I was going to miss the whole day, and all the gossip. But Alex was determined to get us back here in time so he made a few calls and here I am.'

'Yay! Well, we've done the steam room, massages and mani-pedis, I'm afraid...' Poppy pulled round a chair for Lara to sit on. 'All that's left is an hour or so before we head out to meet the guys. But you haven't missed any dirt and we've only just started on the bubbly. Good time?'

'Fabulous. Oh, my God, the hotel was to die for. Alex really knows the best places. We didn't do much, just a lot of relaxing...' Lara's hand went to her belly in a sort of unconscious protective gesture that Poppy thought a little odd. Perhaps she had indigestion. 'But I'm so glad I made it here in time. I wouldn't have missed this for the world.'

'And we're chuffed you made it, too.' They were all back together again. With a huge warm fuzzy in her heart Poppy looked round at her friends. So good to know that even though they were all half of a couple they still prioritised time for each other. And even though Lara was new to the group she was definitely one of them now. Not just because she had fabulous taste, was a brilliant designer and made the most exquisite lingerie—which reminded Poppy, perhaps she needed to do a little investing of her own...or would that breach the new no-clothes policy? Isaac could hardly complain though...could he, if she was naked in satin and lace?

She resolved to stop thinking about him. Again. 'Everyone's got a killer tan. Should I get a spray before the bridesmaid duties?'

Izzy snorted. 'I haven't got one and I'm the bride. Don't you dare turn up orange at my wedding.'

'Anything's got to be better than sickly winter white. Surely? No? Okay, I won't. I promise.' Noticing Lara's empty hands, Poppy remembered her manners. 'Hey, sorry, do you want some champagne? I'll grab a glass from the cabinet for you.'

'No. It's fine, thanks, I'll just stick to water. Jet lag, you know.' Lara held up her robe. 'Where's the changing room?'

'Jet lag? Are you sure? Not a cheeky hangover from your holiday? Hair of the dog will help you feel better.

Come on, everyone has to drink on a sten night. Hag's rules.' Izzy pushed a bowl over to her. 'Nuts? Nibbles? We didn't order too much food because we're going to eat at that restaurant next to Blue later. Plus we need to save room for the cocktails.'

'Er...no.' Lara looked a little uncomfortable. In fact she seemed to visibly pale underneath her tan. Then, looking more than uncomfortable, she hot-footed it to the Ladies. 'Oh, God. Sorry.'

They all looked towards the door and pretended not to hear her throwing up.

'Jet lag?' Tori took another sip of the bubbles. 'It never does that to me. Strange.'

Poppy smiled as the penny dropped. It didn't take a junior gynaecologist to work this out. 'Not strange. Natural. Under the circumstances.'

Perfectly plucked and waxed eyebrows peaked. 'What? You don't think? She's not...? Could she be...?'

'Pregnant?' Lara stood in the doorway, running a glass of water across her forehead. For someone who'd just had her head down a toilet bowl she looked remarkably pleased with herself. 'Yes. Yes, I am! Sorry. I wasn't going to say anything until twelve weeks, but heck...how can I keep a secret from you lot?'

A zillion more group hugs and not a little squealing ensued. Poppy pulled away and looked at Lara—there were a few shadows under her eyes now she'd got closer, and her boobs had grown already. But she had a big nervous smile. 'Wow. That's fabulous news! Oh, my God. A baby!'

'I know. Weird, huh? A little surprised, but we're thrilled.'

'I can give you the lowdown on maternity services at the local hospital and I know some excellent midwives— remind me later. Oh, my God. Alex is going to be a dad. Now that's scary.' Poppy squeezed Lara into another hug.

'No, it's not. It's wonderful. He'll be a great dad—a whole lot better than the one we were saddled with. And you're right, there's no way you could keep that secret from us.' Inwardly Poppy squirmed; she was the one doing a lot of secret keeping from her friends.

They settled down, clucked around Lara a bit more, brought her another glass of iced water, then Izzy clapped her hands. 'Okay, now everyone's here it's game time. Truth or dare.'

'Oh, no-o-o.' Poppy groaned, hoping like hell it would never get to be her turn. It was one thing to lie by omission—after all, no one had ever outright asked if she'd slept with Isaac, or their school teacher, so she'd never volunteered the facts. But it was another thing altogether to openly lie to their faces. She knew she was living on borrowed time.

Lara grabbed the empty bubbles bottle. 'Let the bottle decide the victim.'

'No-o-o.' Still squirming, Poppy retreated further into her seat. It was no use, though; they played this game every time they got a chance—usually with hilarious results.

Tori laughed. 'Hey, last time we played you got me to dish the dirt on my ex, which was pretty embarrassing, so you can at least allow me a chance to get my own back.'

Poppy swallowed another mouthful of bubbly then said, 'He needed dumping ,though. He was so not right for you.'

'Amen to that.' Izzy clinked Tori's glass. 'Good riddance.'

Tori nodded. 'And I guess I did learn that I was going about relationships all the wrong way. You were right—although I didn't think it at the time. You have to give something, too, not just take. See, these games are good therapy and lots of fun. Now, let's do it.'

Poppy didn't need therapy. Isaac had spelt out exactly

what he was prepared to give—she just had to decide whether to keep taking it or not.

See? She was the one in control.

Lara put the bottle on the floor and spun it around. As it whirled past each one of them they, in turn, hauled their feet off the floor with squeals of, 'Not me. Please not me.'

Poppy held her breath as the bottle spun more slowly. Past Lara again. Past Izzy. Even more snail-like past Tori. Until...

Tori looked at her. 'Okay, Pops. Truth or dare?'

Oh, God. She hated this. She remembered a dare that had ended with her having to run naked through the dorm. Aged thirteen. All breast buds and puppy fat. Almost the most humiliating event of her life. The sneering laughter of the older girls rang in her ears even now. That was not happening again.

'Truth.' How bad could it be? Tori wouldn't make things difficult.

'Okay. Let me think. Let me think—'

'I know. I know,' Lara interjected. 'Here's one! Have you ever...ever had sex with someone you shouldn't?'

They all fell silent for a second. All eyes on Poppy while her heart rate tripped into arrhythmia. Izzy cleared her throat and said in a voice that intimated that Lara should surely know this, but they'd all excuse her because she was new. And had pregnancy brain. 'Poppy doesn't have sex. Full stop.'

Lara gasped. 'Really? I know that's what everyone says, but I thought they must be exaggerating. You must have. Surely?'

Everyone says. Poppy winced. Since when was her private life a subject of general debate?

Tori's eyes widened. 'Okay. That's enough, it's fine. Let's move on.'

Poppy looked round at her friends in turn and thought

about everything they'd been through together. How they were always open and honest—no secrets. No regrets.

Even Lara, who was new to them all, had embraced their openness and shared her most private news. And yet she, Poppy, had always carried this hard lump of darkness around with her and it had tainted everything. Had had such an effect on her life for the last ten years that only now was she starting to actually live a full life again.

But instead of feeling fresh and rejuvenated she was making Tori cover up one thing for her, just as she'd made Isaac carry another secret around for a decade.

She couldn't keep doing this. The lies were piling up and dragging her down. Soon everyone would know something about her, but not everything, and she'd be in such a muddle remembering who knew what. Worse—she'd keep on feeling damned sick about it all, too. 'Actually I do need to tell you something. If I don't confess now and get this whole thing out in the open I think I'll explode. It's been eating me up for a long, long time.'

Tori shook her head. 'No, Poppy, you don't have to. It's your own private business. You don't have to say a thing.' Clearly she meant the Isaac sex.

'Yes, she does. Gory deets. Now.' Izzy laughed. 'You bloody dark horse.'

'Okay.' She took a deep breath. It was a lot harder than she'd thought. Finding the words. 'You remember Mr Gantry. Chemistry teacher at school?'

Izzy frowned. 'Yes…'

Lara shook her head. 'No.'

Izzy filled her in. 'Tall. Thin, youngish, about thirty. Sexy in a geeky kind of way, most girls had a crush on him at one time or another; but then, any male teacher in our all-girls' school got a lot of attention. He had floppy hair that fell over his eyes. Jackets with elbow patches. *Married.*'

Poppy looked at the floor and felt the keenness of her shame ripple through her. Even after so long it blew any self-respect away. 'Sorry. This is a downer on a hen night.'

Izzy shook her head. 'Not at all. I'm all ears.'

'Well, we had a thing.'

'At school? A thing? What kind of a thing?'

Poppy felt as if she'd been punched in the gut. 'We had sex. I would say relationship, but it wasn't. Not in the end.'

'You had sex with a teacher?'

Cheeks blazing, Poppy nodded. 'And a lot of sleazy pashing in his car down creepy dark alleys. In the chemistry lab at school, too, when he was supposed to be coaching me in extra lessons so I could get to med school.'

Izzy's eyes were huge. 'What? I'm in shock. You? Sex? What about his wife? Kids?'

'He didn't have any children, although he does now.' She huffed out a deep breath—and she hoped he showered them and his wife with affection and love. Hoped that having children and that extra responsibility might have changed him. 'He told me that he and his wife were living separate lives, that they didn't have sex, that he was going to leave her. For me. And I guess I chose to believe him.' She paused and looked at their open-mouthed expressions. Yes. It was shocking. Dirty. Shameful. 'Then I saw her in the toilets at the Leavers' Ball, overheard her telling another teacher they were so thrilled about her pregnancy. That they'd had difficult times and he'd been a little distant, but things were so good for them now. How much she loved him. They were planning to renew their wedding vows. I'm hoping he did and that he stuck to them.'

Tori's hand covered hers. 'God, how awful. Poor you.'

No. Not any more. Not since that heart-sickening moment of absolute shining clarity had she let herself fall prey to any man's words or charms. If anything the experience had shaped her. Made her stronger in some ways. More determined. Never had she allowed herself to get swept away on another silly teenage hormone-fuelled fantasy. Never again. She shook her head. 'Poor her, more like. In hindsight I had a lucky escape. He was manipulative, creepy. A liar who pretty much damaged any faith I had in men or relationships. But I promised myself then I'd concentrate fully and absolutely on my studies.'

'And you didn't tell anyone about this at all? Even when you were hurting? You must have been hurting. Afterwards?'

Poppy shrugged, trying to be nonchalant when she knew this admission could possibly hurt her friends. She hadn't told them, but she'd told someone else. 'Isaac knows.'

'Isaac? Isaac Blair? What the hell has Isaac got to do with anything?'

Quite a lot in the end. It seemed everything pretty much started and ended with him right now. 'Alex bribed him to be my date for the ball, although for me he was just a smokescreen for the real deal, Gantry. After I showed little interest in Isaac he slunk outside and hung around talking to some guys. Meanwhile I hovered round the disco to catch alone time with Mr Chemistry, drinking surreptitiously from a vodka bottle in my bag, thinking I was so sophisticated. Isaac found out the whole story when he saw me running from the hall in floods of tears. He held my hair while I vomited into the bushes. Listened as I drunkenly blurted out how much I loved Mr bloody Gantry. How I'd been duped and groomed and led on while all the time he was obviously still in love with his wife.'

And again she realised she'd spent a good part of her life avoiding Isaac because he'd seen her at her weakest. He *knew* her like no one else. Knew what she'd done and every time she saw him she'd relived the shame, living in fear he'd tell everyone. But he hadn't and he had never

ever called her on it or cast any blame to anyone other than Gantry.

Score one to Isaac.

Actually, score a lot to Isaac—he'd saved her from mortifying humiliation and hovered in the background of her life quietly making sure she was okay. She owed him more than she could say.

Izzy's voice lowered and, as in all times of stress, her northern accent rippled through her words. 'Seems like Isaac's done you a massive honour by keeping quiet. God knows what Alex would have done if he'd found out. But I wish you'd felt like you could tell us. We would have backed you. You know that, right?'

Guilt ripped through her. 'Of course, of course. But I was so ashamed of myself I couldn't admit it to anyone else and I swore him to absolute secrecy. It's so sordid. I'm so ashamed even now.'

'Well, you don't need to be. Gantry was in the wrong. He was the teacher. The authority figure. You should have reported him.'

Poppy shuddered at the thought. 'And put myself under that kind of spotlight? Imagine how my mother and father would have reacted to that. It was hard enough to get them to give me any kind of love and affection as it was. Something like this would have alienated them completely.' Which, as it turned out, would have mattered little in the end. Her relationship with her parents had remained fractured and distant, anyway. Something she'd come to terms with now. 'I suppose that's part of why I was attracted to Gantry. He was interested in *me*. Wanted *me* out of all the girls there. Or so I thought. But the hard lesson I learnt was that he was only interested in himself all along. Like all men.' She looked at her three girlfriends, all involved with decent honourable guys, including her brother. 'Well, a lot of men. Okay, some men. A few. Maybe a couple.'

Izzy came in for a hug. 'One day you'll find a good one, too. In the meantime you've got us.'

'Thanks. Hag.'

Silence stretched as the girls took all this new information in. She'd expected a backlash of sorts. Blame like that she'd heaped upon herself over the years, more to fuel her shame, but she got none. Just concerned smiles and hugs. And a strange release of all the destructive pent-up guilt. If she'd known she was going to get this reaction she'd have told them years ago. But she'd been nursing her broken heart, not wanting to open herself up to fresh hurt. Reluctant, too, to face up to the fact she'd been *that girl*. The one who'd willingly stepped into the middle of someone else's marriage. Who'd wanted attention so badly she was willing to make herself and others pay any price.

God, what an admission.

But then—as her friends had rightly pointed out, and Isaac, too—she'd been so young and naive and Mr Gantry had groomed her, had showered her with attention when he should have known better.

Izzy poured everyone another glass of bubbles from a fresh bottle. 'Right, I think we all need this. And no more secrets, okay?'

'No more secrets.' Lara clinked her tumbler.

'No more secrets,' Poppy whispered, and took another large slug of wine. Whether it was the alcohol or purging her soul she didn't know, but suddenly everything seemed just a little bit brighter. Even the thought of Isaac.

The other secret she'd just promised not to have.

Tori was still staring at Poppy, mouth open. 'Wow, well, that certainly set the game off to a heady start. No one's going to beat that.' Leaning closer, she whispered, 'And telling them about the other night will be child's play after this.'

Izzy leaned in. 'The other night? What about it?'

Tori mouthed *sorry* and winced.

But Poppy shook her head. 'Oh, and yes…another thing, while we're at it…I have something else to tell you…' They all stared at her again. The Poppy Show was pretty popular tonight. She felt a swell of affection for them all. Couldn't help smiling. Purging your soul was apparently good for you, and having a fling was nothing to be ashamed of. Wasn't that what Isaac had been telling her? If he didn't mind people knowing, then why should she? She wasn't ashamed; she was invigorated. *In for a penny…* 'Isaac and I are having sex now, too.'

A collective *what?* reverberated around the room.

'Isaac?'

'Wow. Isaac? You…and Isaac? Sex? *You?*'

'About bloody time.'

Her friends' reaction to this news was even more startling than the schoolroom clinches she'd told them about. The squeals almost as loud as the reaction to Lara's baby news. 'Poppy? Are you okay? I mean…'

'A bit sore.' She winked at the staring shocked faces. If it hadn't been so embarrassing this could have been fun. It wasn't often she stupefied her friends. 'But I'm absolutely fine. Fine.'

Then she thought about how hard she'd had to try to be light and cheerful this morning. How much she'd ached to stay with Isaac in that tiny bathroom and never let go. Never walk away from him. Never again see him struggling to let her down gently. Because she'd known that was what he was doing—trying to find kind words to put an end to this crazy sexy fling. And she hadn't wanted it to end so she'd put on the bravest face she'd been able to muster. A tight fist of pain lodged under her ribcage. 'I think.'

Izzy put her glass down. 'But Isaac? Whoa. This is more surprising than old Gantry. Isaac is, well, he's…

unobtainable. Mysterious. Sexy as hell. You do mean our Isaac? Your brother's best friend?'

'Oh, yes. But it's nothing permanent for either of us. Just scratching an itch. And he's great, by the way. In the sack. And the shower...' Wasn't that how people talked about their sex lives? Casually and with no emotion. 'A big kahuna.'

Lara coughed into her water. 'Whoa. Okay. We get the picture. Wow. I'm so glad I didn't miss this, but I really wish I could drink something stronger. You girls certainly know how to rock a hens' night.'

CHAPTER THIRTEEN

'LADIES AND GENTLEMEN, we are gathered here today...'

Poppy dragged her eyes away from the magnificent view of the twilit London skyline, amid drifting swirls of snowflakes, from Harry's rooftop garden and focused on the wedding. *Oh, my God.* None of them would ever have imagined this only a few months ago. The snow made the scene so perfect. As did the mistletoe hanging from the rafters. The giant Christmas tree with no-expense-spared decoration in the corner. The scent of pinecones. The lilt of the bridal march played by a string quartet.

On her right Poppy had Alex and Lara. Alex proud with his staunch military stance and yet softened features of a man in love and expecting a child.

Next to Poppy on her left stood Isaac, hands clasped in front of him. Solemn and serious in the smart charcoal suit that made his eyes darker, deeper. Just looking at him knocked the air from her lungs. She'd managed to keep a civilised distance from him today—but that didn't mean she couldn't wait until they were alone again tonight.

It might be her last chance.

But she'd taken her chances over the past week. Spending every night in either his bed or hers, making love for hours. No questions asked. No complicated conversations. It was just enough to be with each other. Talk about the day. About work. About nothing. It was as if by confessing to her friends she'd given herself permission to let go and have fun. To enjoy him, working their way steadily through his version of the *Kama Sutra*.

Hell, it was fun.

And so for a week there'd been blissful harmony in the flat. Tori had moved out with Matt. Alex and Lara were busy flat-hunting and not asking any questions. Which was surprising—if Alex had an opinion on his best friend dating his sister he certainly hadn't voiced it to Poppy. Yet.

Work was going well. Poppy had never felt as if her life could be so complete and fulfilled in all aspects.

Apart from the little glimpses of nagging doubt that whispered to her in the dark as she stroked Isaac's back. As she hurriedly got ready for work, or on the journey home. Or between consultations when she had a moment to think. Which inevitably led to questions and more doubts.

That things would unravel. That time was running out. The clock ticked too quickly towards day thirty-one. She had no illusions that she could change him. That would never work. He would never change, and certainly not if he was boxed into a corner. He had to want to fall in love with her.

And Isaac had no intention of falling in love with anyone.

'Take this?' Izzy turned and passed over her exquisite posy of perfect tiny white tulips and chamomile. For a second she held her friend's gaze.

Poppy smiled, nodded, that dratted lump rising in her throat again. She blinked away tears. 'I'm so proud of you. Be happy.'

'I am.' Izzy smiled back; not one doubt flickered across her face. She looked serene and joyful in the simple yet perfect cowl-necked gown designed by Lara, her shoulders covered in a sweet pure white angora cardigan, and surrounded by her family.

Few of Harry's family had made the day, so there would be another wedding celebration in Australia. No doubt a full-on major media event befitting Harry's celebrity status over there. But a lot of his friends were here—and that somehow seemed enough for him. Actually, Poppy got the impression that Harry would have been perfectly happy if no one else had been there at all. Just him, and his beautiful bride.

As they were pronounced man and wife Poppy felt Isaac's warm hand grip hers. The stroke of his thumb along her palm. Heard his regular breathing, so close. She daredn't look at him. Because things had become so intense so quickly, her emotions entwined in the sex and in Isaac so thickly, that she knew her real feelings would be there in her eyes, on display not just to him, but to everyone else, too.

So she squeezed his hand and let it go. Marched towards the wedding party and dragged on her very best, very proud smile. 'Oh, congratulations, Izzy. Harry! Make an honest woman of her? Good luck with that!'

'Do you want to dance? Or go home? Your call.' It was late. The food had been eaten and the drink drunk. The toasts and speeches finished. Now the hangers-on were stepping back and forth to an old slow number in the small area of dance-floor they'd created in the über-fancy restaurant, Ecco. Isaac had spent the day giving Poppy some space to be with her friends, and to revel in the whole wedding marathon, but now he wanted to run his hands over her body. Preferably in bed, but anywhere would do. The sooner the better.

She gazed up at him through long black eyelashes that he knew weren't in any way real. And he didn't care one bit; they accentuated her eyes, made her look innocent and wise at the same time. Which, he supposed, she was.

She looked amazing with her rich dark curls swept up into some sort of loose bun thing, and the dark claret sheath bridesmaid dress enhancing every inch of the curves he knew so well. His heart jolted a little as he realised just how much she made him smile. How much he wanted that smile to keep on happening.

She took his outstretched hand and stood on dark red heels that could easily pierce skin but made her legs longer and leaner, and he fought an urge to run his hand up to her thigh. And beyond. 'One dance? Then we go?'

He pulled her into his arms. 'You look beautiful today.'

'Thank you. And you're not so bad yourself.' She pressed a quick kiss onto his lips. Clearly not embarrassed to be seen with him after all. 'I prefer you without the suit. Well, without clothes in general.'

He led her to the floor and wrapped his arms round her tiny waist, swaying to the soft music, inhaling her perfume, which sent his head into a spin. Would he ever have enough of that scent?

Izzy and Harry swirled by, waving, and Isaac inclined his head towards them. 'A teensy bit jealous of Mr and Mrs?'

Poppy smiled and pressed closer to him. If he didn't know any better he'd have thought she was purposefully rubbing her breasts against his shirt. And for a second he wished he'd whisked her home instead.

'Actually, no. Not at all. Izzy is deliriously happy, but she deserves it all. Every bit of it. They all do. And, wow, Lara and Alex. A baby.' Her eyes widened and he got a glimpse of honeyed caramel flecks in her warm pupils. He hadn't noticed them before. He was learning something new about her all the time. Noticing things. Small things. Things he liked. Things that would be hard to forget. 'I still can't get my head around that.'

'Yeah, well, let's hope he doesn't lose that in Vegas,

like he did his inheritance.' Isaac felt a strange stab of something in his chest. Alex was moving on now, too. Finally becoming the decent adult Isaac had pegged him to be from the start. And a baby. Maybe a son of his own. A wife. Isaac had a sense of being left behind—that there was something missing—yeah, that he was missing out. Which was a whole heap of ridiculous because he had everything he wanted in his business. Stability, security. Success. What more did a man need? He rested his cheek on Poppy's. 'Him, a father! Miracles do happen. It's yet another thing I can rib him about.'

'Don't you dare. It happens to us all in the end,' a voice whispered close to his ear. *Alex.* 'And I'm watching you, matey. You hurt my sister and I'll break your legs.' Then he slapped him on the back with a friendly grin and sailed off across the dance floor with Lara.

Isaac frowned. 'Why does everyone want to break my legs?'

'Because they love me.'

'And what about me?' He couldn't help the smile. He knew Alex was being good-humoured about this thing with Poppy. But there was truth in her brother's threats. Everyone adored her; she was the glue that held the group together and he would never be forgiven for breaking her heart. 'They've known me for just as long. I need my legs. I like them.'

'Me, too.' Her hand went to his thigh and she slowly rubbed it tantalisingly close to his groin. 'Oh, don't worry. They all love you, too. But you do have a reputation, Mr Blair.'

'Excellent. And it's all true. You want to take advantage?' Why was it that each and every time he thought about letting her go he said something to make her stay?

Her eyes sparked heat and excitement and a thick sexual smog enveloped them. Her fingers played with his shirt collar, her touch sending shocks of need through him. 'I think I just might. Tonight I want to pick your brains about whipped cream...'

'You have some?'

She licked her lips, eyes tantalisingly bright and teasing. 'Maybe...'

'Why didn't you say so? Let's go now.' He tried to shut out the thought of her covered in strategic blobs of cream, and of him licking them off. But was glad he failed in any way to stop the image coming into his head.

'Ah, but first Izzy has to throw the bouquet. I have to hang around for that.'

Oh-oh. 'They still do that? I thought it went out in the fifties?'

'It's only a bit of fun. We all promised we'd stay. Look, I think she's going to do it now.'

'Oh. God.' This was the corny part of the wedding ceremony that made him want to run and hide. But he couldn't move too far without his trousers revealing just how turned on she made him. He held her in front of him. And she rubbed her backside against it as the bride took her place in the centre of the dance floor.

He groaned into her hair. 'You don't seem in much of a hurry to catch the flowers.'

She looked ahead at the giggling, jostling huddle of women with their hands in the air, and laughed. 'Don't worry. You're safe. Besides, I'd rather stay right where I am.'

'Me, too. Don't even think about walking away.' He nuzzled her neck and was just about to pull her into a kiss when something sailed towards him and, instinctively, he ducked. Somehow, though, the bouquet landed in his hands.

The watching crowd fell into roars of laughter. Wolf

whistles reverberated off the restaurant walls. He gave them all a rueful grin.

Not knowing what to do, he stared at the posy for a second. What happened now? Should he give them to Poppy? She believed all that hokum about marriage and everlasting love. He didn't want to give her the wrong impression by offering her the flowers. What would she read into that?

But…would it be such a mad idea? Would it be so difficult to relax into something more long term? Like his mates.

He blinked. Whoa. Stupid fantasy. He was already a hypocrite by being here. He didn't believe in ever after. Hadn't seen much evidence of it happening.

And yet…so many people did believe. So many took that leap of faith. People he respected. People who, he knew, might just make it all work. Alex and Lara, Izzy and Harry, Tori and Matt—they all bought into the fairy tale. And, looking at their shining faces, listening to their words, knowing what they'd all overcome to get this far, he knew now they were all going to make it.

Why wouldn't he want a slice of that?

Why wouldn't he even want to try?

Because it was a risk he wasn't prepared to take. It was too much to ask. And these kinds of things did not happen in his world. Marriages didn't last. Promises were broken. Not just once, but over and over.

But, for the record, if he were going to risk his heart on anyone, it would be Poppy Spencer.

For a few long moments she held his gaze. He saw the teasing in her eyes, her relaxed demeanour as she bent forward and picked the bouquet out of his grasp. 'I'll be having these, then.' She laughed and raised them into the air to cheers from the onlookers. 'Don't look so frightened. I won't hold you to it.'

'I thought…perhaps.'

She winked. 'Too much thinking. Now, I have whipped-cream plans…so come on.'

Later when the whipped-cream can was empty and Poppy lay sleeping next to him in her bed, soft sounds coming from her throat, Isaac couldn't shake that commitment thought away. He'd been on the verge of doing something very stupid back there in the restaurant.

And things were getting more complicated as each day passed. He'd never given so much thought to a… relationship. Yep. That was what this was starting to become. No denying that seeing someone every day for breakfast and sleeping with them at night could be called anything other. And this was everything he'd tried to avoid. His whole life. His heart contracted as he saw his life shrinking. As if everything he knew were balancing on a knife's edge and he couldn't stop it from falling. That he was going to be blasted open, raw and vulnerable. Again.

A spike of fear wedged into his ribcage.

He couldn't have her getting the wrong idea, getting used to this set-up. It was temporary. A stopgap. He needed to tell her.

That spike of fear intensified and he didn't know whether it was due to the thought of it ending, or because of the chink in his heart that made him want to stay.

Tossing the covers aside, he decided to get some distance. Some space elsewhere in the dark where she wouldn't be so tempting with her lush hair and her cute mouth. With her funny quips and interesting conversation that held him captive for hours.

She stirred a little, her arm reaching across him. One leg creeping over his as she pressed against his back. 'Where are you going?'

Hell.

He settled back to cuddle her. Starting an early Christmas morning at seven o'clock sucked; she needed some decent sleep. Creating a scene now wouldn't help. Disappearing would be a coward's way out. 'Nowhere. Just a little hot.'

'Do you want to get hotter?' Her fingers stroked along his chest and just that mere feather touch had him wanting her again.

He wouldn't ruin her Christmas. He wouldn't snatch away the happiness. Not yet. He'd wait.

Or was that the coward's way? He should be up-front—make her know that things would be going right back to how they were before. Before...he could barely remember a time when she wasn't in his thoughts.

'Shh.' He stroked her hair, slicked a small kiss on her forehead. 'Later. You've got work tomorrow. We'll catch up after you've caught a dozen screaming babies. You need to sleep.'

'I need you. In me.' She wriggled against him, hand inching over his erection. Her mouth found his and before he knew what he was doing he was inside her again. So easy to want her. To need her right back.

He took a nipple between his fingers, rubbed gently and felt her contract around him. Then sucked the pink bud into his mouth. The nipple puckered and she groaned again, a visceral roar that fired him more. She stabbed her fingers into his hair and pushed against him, deeper. Deeper. Deeper.

He loved this. Loved the feel of her soft skin against his. Loved the dips and curves of her body. Loved the way they were together, instinctively knowing what each other wanted.

He loved... He closed his eyes, refusing to admit the feeling he recognised but had never felt before. It was just the rush of the sex, the crazy day, her. It wasn't anything. Nothing. It wasn't...

No. His heart slammed faster and faster. It wasn't. It couldn't be.

He couldn't allow it. Wouldn't...

When he opened his eyes again she was staring at him, her gaze filled with soft emotion, not the intense spark of sex, but something warmer, deeper. Something more...

He rocked against her deeper still. It would never be deep enough. And yet...

Her arm gripped his shoulders and rocked against him, their rhythm slow, infused with an unhurried intensity as if they had all the time in the world. He tried to commit this feeling to memory. The joy on her face. The soft moan as his lips met hers. Because he couldn't do this again. Not feel these intense emotions for someone so wrong, so precious, so perfect, and know they would never last.

It was a kiss like none he'd ever had before. As if his deepest emotions were suffused in his touch, as if he could see deep inside her. To her heart, her soul. To that precious part of her that was pure and raw and his. If only for this moment.

And he gave himself in return. Lost in her. With her. Because of her.

CHAPTER FOURTEEN

'*WE WISH YOU a Merry Christmas!*' Poppy sang as she carried a tray laden with warm croissants and coffee to her bedroom. When she'd offered to work all day today she hadn't banked on the fact she'd have to leave Mr Sexy Legs here. One of the aforementioned stuck out from the sheets and her gaze followed it all the way from his toes to…the most entertaining part of his body. He was magnificent.

Happy Christmas indeed! They'd certainly seen the dawn through with a bang. The only thing to make it absolutely perfect would be snow. The last fall had melted leaving a sheen of sludge on the pavements that had quickly turned to ice overnight. She peered through the chink in the curtains; the early weak sun was masked by cloud that, in the distance, looked dark and black. Rain-laden. Not snow.

After putting the tray down she sat on the bed and ruffled Isaac's hair. 'I wouldn't have woken you, only I'm going in soon and I wanted to wish you a happy day.'

Jerking awake, he rubbed his eyes and sat up, pooling the duvet across his middle. He had an early-morning frown that made him look less like his laid-back self. 'Er… okay. Thanks. You, too.'

No *happy Christmas*? No suggestion of mistletoe. Nothing different or special. She was fast understanding that

Isaac didn't wear his emotions on his sleeve. But...well, it was Christmas. 'Plans?'

'None.'

Having poured the coffee, she handed him a cup. 'You are going to see your family, aren't you? Surely you don't intend to stay here on your own all day?'

'Maybe.' He paused and took a sip of coffee. 'Unless I can convince you to phone in sick and spend it with me?'

Yes, please. 'Tempting, but no. It's no good if the doctor phones in sick, is it? Who's going to help deliver all those lovely Christmas babies today?' And, in truth, part of her wanted to be in the thick of things at the hospital where she could see the joy on people's faces on this special day. Working took her attention off the numerous 'what ifs' that had taken root in her head. And that were being amplified right now by the frown and the distinct lack of any kind of festive spirit.

She tried to focus on the conversation and distract herself. 'You need to go see them.'

'I don't need to do anything. I'm sure they won't miss me.'

'Of course they will. It's Christmas. Give her a chance.'

He stroked a finger down her arm. 'And you'd know all about it, would you? Seeing as you're going to work right now instead of taking a trip back home yourself.'

He had a point. Mummy and Daddy had issued their usual last-minute emotionless invitation but she was busying herself through the day, and seeing Alex later—he was really all the family she truly cared about. And that was okay.

Isaac, on the other hand, was doing nothing and she hated to think of him lonely and miserable. Especially when she knew his mother had asked him to visit and he was conflicted. 'But everyone deserves another go. Surely?'

'I'm not so sure I share your optimism. Everyone? Even people like Tony Gantry? You think?'

Tension prickled through her—but it was noticeably less than whenever she'd thought about her old teacher before. 'I hope his family have a good Christmas, even if I don't want him to have a good one ever. By the way, I told the girls about him. It was quite a relief actually. I think I've finally made my peace with that phase of my life. It felt good.'

'You told them about Gantry. Why? After all this time?'

'I'm sick of hiding it away. I think the only way of moving forward is to acknowledge my mistakes and be open to making new ones. I've decided I want to live a full life, not a half one.' She sucked in air and as she threw him the next comment she watched for his reaction. 'I want to have relationships. I want to fall in love. Like everyone else.'

He shook his head and frowned again, this time more deeply. Not exactly the response she'd hoped for. 'You sound more like Izzy every day. What happened to practical, logical Poppy?'

She fell in love.

Wham.

The realisation was like a sledgehammer to her chest and she inhaled sharply at the thought, clutched the corner of the sheet tight between her fingers.

She loved him.

Even after she'd worked hard not to. When she'd thought she was in control and calling the shots. She cared for him. Wanted him. Wanted him to be happy. Couldn't bear the thought of another moment without him in her life. If that meant she loved him. Then yes.

But telling him? God, no.

And yet...she'd changed so much through these past few weeks. Because of him she now knew she wanted more. Something meaningful. Something sustainable. She wanted to be loved, too.

And right there. *There.* She imagined how wonderful it would be if this would continue. If they stopped pretending, and got real. She wanted to be surrounded by love like the new parents at work, and her friends—even to have a baby of her own one day. She wanted it all. More frightening still, she wanted it with Isaac.

So being naked in bed with a gloriously sexy man who didn't know commitment from his elbow was so not the time to acknowledge this. 'Logical Poppy's still there. She just thinks that it might be possible to want it all—and have it. Why not? Alex has it. Izzy. Tori.'

'Nah. You just bought into the fairy tale, got carried away by the dress and the bling and the bouquet.'

And he was the wrong man to fall in love with. 'You think? Am I really so shallow? It's not just because they're doing it—don't be ridiculous. That would be idiotic. But I do know that they're happy and fulfilled.' And she'd had a slice of the same these past few weeks and knew that if she'd experienced a fraction of the feelings they had, then it had been worth it. But she wanted it to last. A large chunk of sadness filled her gut. 'It makes everything worthwhile in the end, all the struggles and the hard work to get to the top. Why have a career if you can't share that success with someone? Don't you think?'

He shrugged and his eyes flashed both a dare and a threat. 'How would I know?'

'Have you given it a chance? Like ever? Instead of running away from every scrap of feelings why don't you try to live through it?' She reached for his hand. 'What happened to you?'

His eyes narrowed. 'Nothing. I'm just a natural-born cynic.'

'No, you're not. You choose to believe that some good

things can happen. Like your business. Like...fun times with your friends. Even with me. You choose to invest in half of life but shun the other half. The good bit where you get the chance to be deeply happy.'

He scraped a hand across his stubbled jaw. 'I would never rely on someone else to make me happy. I can manage that perfectly well on my own.'

The words stung like a slap. He could sit here and lie all he liked but she knew he was different when he was with her. She saw the smiles, couldn't deny the laughter. And the sex—that was way more than fun. It meant something. And he knew it. He was just hedging. Running scared.

Anger mixed with sadness in her gut. 'Well, good for you. But it doesn't have to be like that. You just have to take a risk.' Glancing at the clock, she realised she was going to be late if she didn't leave now. But she couldn't go. Not yet. 'You ever think that just maybe the poets, the writers, the film makers, and millions and millions of people who settle down and have families might be right? That you can have it all? I repeat...what happened to you?'

She hiked up from the bed and threw on some clothes, twisted her hair into a knot and clipped it in place at the back of her head. Slipped on her shoes and with them an irritated tone to her voice. 'Go ahead and talk, Isaac. I'm dressed and ready to leave but I'm not going anywhere yet. Because right now I think this is more important. And, well—putting something else before work—that's a huge thing for me.'

He straightened in the bed. Looked everywhere else but at Poppy. 'For God's sake, you know damned well what happened. She traded one husband for another, then another. Worse, she traded one family for another. Have you any idea how that feels? When your mum prefers another kid to you? Holds them up as paragons of bloody virtue, a fresh start, a clean slate, and treats you like you're the devil incarnate. Because you're an inconvenience. Because you've lost your way and got into a bit of trouble. Police trouble—but not enough for juvenile centre. Just enough to make her embarrassed. And suddenly you don't fit her standards or her expectations.'

'Actually I do know exactly how it feels not to fulfil parental expectations. Alex and I have been a huge inconvenience to our parents our whole lives. That's normal for us. But it isn't for you—you had a good relationship with her once. Didn't you?' At the nod of his head she continued, 'It might be hard but I suggest you try to get over those kinds of things.'

He pointed to her work clothes, his face incredulous. 'Yeah? Like you do? So you're working today instead of going home. And for eight years you've hidden away from relationships, haven't acted on any kind of whim. Have kept secrets from your family because you've been ashamed of something you did a decade ago. That kind of *get over it*?'

'We're talking about you, not me.'

'Thanks, but I don't need to spill my guts about my mother. It doesn't make me feel better. It's just enough for you to know that I learnt from a young age never to seek any affirmation from anyone else and to be absolutely self-reliant.'

'Well, you certainly perfected that.' She looked around, wondering what to do next. What to say. He'd made up his mind to be distant and single for the rest of his life, wouldn't even entertain any idea otherwise.

She thought about how difficult it would have been to be a teenager in the midst of all that pubertal angst of discovering who he was—and to be rejected by the one person who should love him unconditionally. At least, that was how he saw it. Poppy was convinced his mum must have a different view. Because wasn't she now a devoted mother of two boys? In a successful sustained marriage? Hadn't she invited him back for Christmas? There was hope there.

Poppy also thought about how much she owed him, over the years, for holding her dirty secret close to his chest. For watching out for her. For noticing.

Her heart contracted at the thought that he'd been there all the time and she'd refused to notice him. Had kept her distance from him. 'For the record, I'm proud of how you turned out. You are successful and kind and loyal. All qualities I admire. For some reason I was always wary of the fact you knew the worst thing about me. But thank you for keeping my secret, Isaac. It's the best thing anyone's ever done for me.'

'For all the good it did. I just colluded in a web of secrecy that stunted you emotionally. You should have reported him.' He held his finger up. 'No. I should have hit the bastard.'

'Thank God you didn't.'

'I would have enjoyed it.'

She gave him a smile. 'It would certainly have been another thing to annoy your mother with.'

'Like she needed an excuse.' He looked at the clock by the bed and let out a deep breath. The shadows in the crevasses of his cheeks made him look tired. Haunted. 'Look, Poppy, time's ticking on. This is going nowhere.'

'What is?' Panic gripped her throat; she swallowed it down. She'd always known there would be an end. She'd just hoped she'd make it to day thirty-one.

'You should go. You're going to be late.'

'I already am. And you should go home, Isaac. Talk to her. Learn about her, give her a chance. Is she happy? Does she love him? Will they make it in the long haul? Perhaps, long ago she was confused and chose the wrong men—but that doesn't mean she hasn't found the right man now. Who knows? Maybe they have an unshakeable understanding, maybe they're soul mates. Maybe she does love you but doesn't know what to do about it now?'

Like me. She pressed a kiss to his lips and hoped she showed him just a little bit of how much she felt for him. That there was at least one person who loved him. For whatever good it would do her.

Something in his dark withdrawn expression told her she would not get the chance to do this again. That this was the end. That she had got from Isaac the most he had ever given to anyone. But that was it—he could give no more.

A chill as cold as the outside air ran through her. She wanted to wrap herself around him. But she had to go. Suspecting he wouldn't be here when she got back cut through her like a scalpel blade. 'Let me know how you get on. Text me?'

He nodded. 'Don't hold your breath.'

'About what? The progress...or the text?' She wished she hadn't brought him this tray. Hadn't woken up on a day so laden with pressure that she'd thought she might find something to make her happy. Wished she hadn't fallen in love with Isaac Blair. Wished wholeheartedly now that she hadn't probed into a deep conversation that reminded him of how little faith he had in love and relationships.

'Look, Poppy...'

No. Don't say it.

He didn't need to. She could see what was coming, heard it, felt the heavy vibrations of rejection like an out-of-control juggernaut bearing down on her, and if she could have blocked her ears like an eight-year-old she would have. Tears pricked at the backs of her eyes. She blinked them away, because she sure as hell wasn't going to show him how much this was hurting. 'What?'

Isaac inhaled, trying to choose the right words; the pain in his heart twisted tightly as he watched her smiling face crumble. She'd been expecting this, probably all along—

waiting for the cards to fall. But even he hadn't expected it to cut so deep. Hadn't expected to fall so hard for her. To care so much. Such pain was a shock. And although last night, last week he'd decided to end it, waking up to her this morning was the finest Christmas present he'd ever had.

The best way to do this was to cut ties now before things got messy. To go away somewhere and leave her to get over him. Then, to keep at the far edge of her circle of friends, to lie low where he could watch over her, make sure she was okay but keep a distance. Moving on. Which she would—she'd grown so much. Poppy was a beautiful, strong and independent woman. He only wished he had half her fortitude. To try. To love. To open himself up to risk.

The pain twisted harder. He couldn't think about her moving on with another man, someone who would love and cherish her. But she deserved someone who could give her what he couldn't.

Isaac's hand was on her hair, stroking it. His fingers loosening the tight knot. But he wasn't seducing her. He was saying sorry. His mind made up. A plan formulated. And okay, some might say it was running away...he just needed a clean break. They both did. 'I have to go to Paris soon. Maybe tomorrow. There's stuff happening. Problems with the electrics that Jamie couldn't get to the bottom of. I need to fix them. I could be there a while. I don't know when I'll be back...'

Bile burnt the back of Poppy's throat. Of all the rotten, stinking times to ruin her day he'd chosen this one? 'Have to go, or want to go?'

Don't say it.

But he looked away and she had her answer.

Both.

Silence stretched between them. She wanted to press against his body and keep him here. Wanted him to want to stay. To want her enough—to want *this* enough—to take a risk. Wanted to hear him say it. But instead he said nothing. And she would never ever beg. Or even ask.

Eventually she found what was left of her self-respect and her voice and croaked out a response. 'Okay. So send me a postcard, if they even exist any more. And I'd appreciate the rent in advance…but if you want to just pack up and leave then that's fine, too. I'll put an advert on the hospital noticeboard—'

'Poppy—'

'Paris is lovely. Lucky you. Of course, work. Yes. Work comes first for us career people.' She waved her hand at him, more to stop herself stroking her fingers down that beautiful bare chest, or pressing her hand to his cheek, than anything else. She couldn't touch him again. Not now. It would make things so much worse. 'It's fine. Really. I'll just need to find some more flatmates. The mortgage won't pay itself. Of course, I'll reword the flatmate policy…wouldn't want the whole naked thing going on with strangers… Stupid, really, to think…hope. Anyway, I really should just go to work. I'm going to be very late. I wonder how many Hollys and Noels we get today…'

He took her hand. 'Pops, stop. I'm sorry.'

'No need. We both knew. An end, you know. That's okay. Got to go to work. Happy Christmas.' She shook her hand out of his grip. Couldn't bear the feel of his skin against hers when it was goodbye.

Oh, God. The words, the thoughts, the emotions pierced her to her core—a sharp, glittering hurt that stabbed hard in her ribcage.

She loved him and he didn't love her back.

Loved him.

Of all the foolhardy, stupid things to do. The worst kind of stupid because he'd always be around somewhere—with Alex, with her friends, smiling, maybe with a new girlfriend, reminding her of what she'd had and could never have again. Being there. Breaking her heart every single time.

Somehow she left him there, in her bed. Somehow she walked away, closed the front door and strode down the steps, head held high. Somehow she got to work, dragged on a brave face and delivered two Hollys, a Gabriel and a Star. Somehow she laughed at the wonder of birth and new life and cried happy tears with the parents.

But later, after a quick crying-off to Alex and Lara on the pretext of a migraine, she crawled under the covers and inhaled Isaac's smell. She wrapped herself in sheets that had barely covered them both. Nuzzled her face in his pillow.

She lay in the dark empty room in her lonely apartment and wondered why the hell she had let herself do something so heartbreakingly stupid, something so spectacularly un-Poppy-like? Something so catastrophically crazy as thinking that she could have sex without emotion over and over again with a man like Isaac Blair. How she could share fears and dreams. Develop a sensual self-confidence from his tutelage—feel a sense of contentment. A part of something. Important. Special. Precious. How just breathing the same air as one man could feel rarefied and unique. How his laughter could infect her. His touch. Smell.

Why had she allowed herself to experience every emotion with him? Especially when she knew from the start he was incapable of doing the same.

Isaac fell back against the pillow and groaned. *Stupid bastard.*

Stupid. Dumb. Goddamn stupid.

If he hadn't believed this was the totally right thing to do he could have been convinced it was the far side of madness.

He'd watched the only woman he'd ever allowed himself to care for slip away—holding back her tears, trying hard to convince him that this was the best decision he'd ever made. That she didn't care. That everything was fine.

It wasn't fine.

And he'd let her go. On Christmas Day. The magic... gone. That was something he could never make up to her. He'd ruined her day.

But the feelings she stoked in him left him adrift, clamouring for some kind of anchor. His world tipped sideways as letting her go seemed right but keeping her close felt righter. His heart raced. His gut churned. He was hot and cold. And, yes...panicked. And he'd seen the light in her eyes blink out.

It *would* be fine. She'd get over him in time. She had a forgiving heart and she'd understand that what he'd done was the right thing to do after all. For them both. It just might take him a whole lot longer. Maybe a lifetime.

Three hours later a different kind of irritation rattled up Isaac's spine. Today he was the king of bad ideas. Christmas dinner had been difficult, conversation stilted. The only saving grace had been the two boys, who'd loved the gifts he'd brought them. But then, you couldn't go wrong with remote-control helicopters.

He was standing at the large bow window overlooking the manicured lawn, watching Archie and Henry run around screaming and playing with the remote controls. The sky hung heavily with thick dark clouds, threatening to pour with rain. No snow yet. Poppy would be disappointed.

And yes, every thought came back to her.

His mother, smiling beatifically in a powder-blue couture dress, stood next to him. She gave him a smile. And he thought that for once it might be genuine. 'You're good with them. They like you.'

He nodded. 'I like them, too.'

'I remember when you were that age—'

'What do you remember, Mum? Because I was at boarding school most of the time, and you were pretty distracted most holidays.' He knew exactly what he remembered. An affair. Secrets. Hushed voices. Divorce.

Then being whisked away from the place he'd made his home and sent to the local college. And still she was distracted. Another marriage. Then another one. Drama. Always drama. Raised voices. Then Hugo, and a step-brother. Then a baby. And it all seemed so removed from his reality and he didn't fit anywhere. He'd looked on from a distance in detached bemusement.

That was what he'd thought. But in reality he'd crushed the pain and sunk his head into other things. Getting into trouble. Bars. Drinking. Then a friendship that led to a business partnership. Making his first thousand dollars. Ten thousand. A million.

And still his mother's lack of interest. He'd reached the point where he didn't bother to contact her from one Christmas to the next. And then this year she'd reached out.

She stared out of the window, but she seemed to be fixed on nothing in particular. Just a spot somewhere on the horizon. 'I wasn't a good mother to you, Isaac. And for that I'm very sorry. I know I could have done better.'

He shrugged, shoving his hands in his pockets. 'I understand.'

'No, you don't. And I don't really, either. I was young when you were born and trapped in an unhappy marriage. I didn't want you to feel that, so I sent you away to school to shield you from it. I hoped you'd be happier. I tried to make things work. They didn't. Then I tried again. And failed. I'm used to being a failure. I guess Hugo and these boys have been my biggest success. This marriage.' *Man, that stung.* 'I'm sorry you weren't part of it. I am so very proud of you, though.'

Yeah? 'Now. Maybe.'

'Yes, now. Not always, but I just wasn't looking for things to be proud of back then.' She turned to face him, handed him a glass of brandy she'd poured from a decanter. 'Do you have a girlfriend?'

'No.'

'Shame. I always imagined you'd be the kind to settle. You like stability. I realise that now. I should have given you that. I hope you find it.'

'I have my work.' He took a sip, felt the sting of heat and the rush through his body. 'I'm good on my own. I don't need it.'

She patted his arm. First real contact he'd had from her in for ever. 'We all need someone, Isaac. Even you. What the hell do you think I was doing all those years? Finding someone I could truly love. Who I wanted to stay with regardless of age, or money, or…anything. Someone who I wanted to be with night and day. Who I couldn't bear to be without. Who I wanted to do things for, who I wanted to make happy. And who could love me back the same way.'

'And did you? Find him in the end?' He heard his step-father's voice from the kitchen, singing a Christmas carol Isaac had learnt at boarding school. The atmosphere in this home was so different from when he'd grown up. Archie and Henry were lucky. 'Or is Hugo likely to be yet another version of Mr Wrong?'

'He's—what do you call it these days?—a keeper. You just have to keep looking, Isaac, and realise, when you find them, that they're worth fighting for.'

Could he really believe her? He seriously doubted it was worth the effort. The drama. The heartache. Although, Poppy…

He glanced outside at the kids on the lawn, the smile on

his mother's face, the feeling of contentment in this place. He could have had that. He could have had what Alex had. He could have had Poppy. It was all within his grasp.

His gut tightened against more brandy. He didn't want to go there—to relive the biggest mistake of his life. Because Poppy *was* worth the drama and the effort. He just hadn't realised. And now he hadn't a clue how to fix it. And then there was that flight to Paris tomorrow and the open-ended ticket with no return date...

He shook his head, not knowing whether his mother was telling the truth; maybe you did just have to realise what was worth fighting for. It had taken her years of searching. Was that what he had in store for him? Years of wilderness? She looked happy now, content. She certainly looked as if she meant every word.

Either that or she was sozzled on the cooking sherry.

CHAPTER FIFTEEN

'But you always have a New Year's Eve party, Poppy? Come on.' Tori resecured one earring, then the other, then turned to Poppy in the pub's bathroom where they were fixing their make-up. 'We can text everyone and get them to meet us back at yours. It just won't be the same in Trafalgar Square. It's heaving with crowds already.'

Poppy sighed. Yes. That was the plan. So she could lose herself in the masses. 'We've fought our way through endless queues of people to get this far. The square's just around the corner. New Year, new start. I'm wiping the slate clean. Besides, the fireworks will be awesome. I only ever see them on TV.'

Tori stopped mid-mascara touch-up. 'You know, I'm just a little bit scared by you right now. You've changed. You're selling the flat from under our feet. You've booked a holiday to Mexico—'

'First off, I am not selling it from under your feet—you don't even live there any more. No one does but me. And the occasional mouse. All my chicks have left the nest, and Alex needs somewhere for his family. It makes sense to sell it to him and move on. There are too many memories there. It's about time I freed myself up financially. I want to live more, experience things. Lots of things…' Apart from another broken heart. She could do without that. But Isaac had awakened a sense of adventure in her that she wanted to explore. It was her time now, no more hiding herself away...

Just as soon as she fixed back the shattered pieces of her heart.

Poppy snapped her lips together, setting her new red lipstick. Truth was, she didn't want a party in her apartment where she would be the only single loose part. She wanted to be surrounded by thousands of people counting down to midnight. When the weird Isaac spell would be broken and she would turn back into her usual sensible, professional self. Normal service would be resumed. And she would start anew. Selling the apartment was the first step in her plan.

'He's not worth it, Pops.' Tori's eyes misted. 'If he doesn't know a good thing when he's got it.'

'It was never meant to be long term. I knew that going in.' She had her friends, her job, a future and freedom on the horizon—what more could she need? Ignoring the voice that whispered in her head...*Isaac*, she pulled on her hat and fastened her scarf, tucked her arm into Tori's thick woollen-coated one. Fixed on a smile. 'Let's go. Come on, next year's just around the corner. It's going to be so exciting.' And who knew, if she said it enough she might start to actually believe it.

An icy blast of air hit them as they stepped outside. Swirls of tiny snowflakes drifted from the sky and she smiled.

Thousands, maybe hundreds of thousands, of people surged alongside them towards the square; everyone had pink cheeks and big grins. The noise of happy chatter filled the night. Busier than she'd ever seen it before, the place was so congested there were huge LED signs detailing up-to-date road closures, safety notices and, every few minutes, a countdown to midnight.

Twelve minutes.

Heart racing, she linked arms with Lara and Tori and headed towards the fun, leaving the complex heart-aching emotions of this year behind her.

Well, almost.

Eleven minutes.

Isaac glanced at the blasted electronic display and cursed. The plane had been delayed by a snowstorm, which appeared to have caught them up, judging by the cold wet drifting down his neck. The tube had been an almost impossible crush and he'd run the length of Haymarket to get here. Ridiculous. The chances of finding her were minuscule. Impossible. But he forged ahead. She was here, Alex's text had said. Trafalgar Square. She was here.

Ten minutes.

Trying to keep his heart rate in check, he climbed a bollard. Every woman with long dark hair could be her. Every lyrical laugh. Every group of people could be her and her friends. But they weren't. So many people with streamers and glow-in-the-dark wristbands and every type of celebratory paraphernalia for sale. But he just wanted one thing. Poppy.

Damn. This was ridiculous.

Eight minutes.

Another bloody sign. He fought back an urge to kick the damned thing. Annoying, useless piece of technology stating the damned obvious and blocking his view.

Where the hell was she?

* * *

'I think here's a great place.' Poppy stopped when they could get no closer to the centre of the square. Revellers were already dancing in the fountains, practising 'Auld Lang Syne' with varying amounts of success—did anyone ever know the right words? All around them there was a wall of noise, of music, of singing. Strangers shared food, drinks and smiles. The buzz and high-energy atmosphere were infectious.

'Not exactly intimate, but it'll do.' Alex nodded and wrapped his arms around Lara. She smiled up at him. Matt grabbed Tori in for a hug. Poppy looked on, wishing Izzy were here instead of in Australia. Then at least they'd all be together. But there would be other times, plenty of times, when they would all be together again.

Her heart squeezed. Maybe coming here had been one of her worst ideas. Because no matter where she was, she wasn't anywhere with Isaac.

Ahem, what about that new start?

Today was the beginning. She took a moment, like the others, to gaze around at a snow-filled sky that she knew would soon be lit up by a rainbow of fireworks. Beside her, silent and watching disdainfully, a dark stone lion sat at the feet of the immense Nelson's column. God knew what he made of it all. She ran her fingers down the cool stone. 'Bet you'd make a fine mouse-catcher, my man. Fancy a job?'

Six minutes, a screen close by told her. It flickered again. New words formed.

URGENT: DR SPENCER CHECK YOUR PHONE

Then it was gone just as quickly, replaced by another announcement about congestion.

What? Poppy blinked, a tight catch in her ribcage. 'Did you see that?'

Matt nodded. '*You* Dr Spencer? Did it mean you? Check your phone.'

She couldn't drag her gloves off quickly enough. Five missed calls.

Isaac.

The noise all around her had masked her ringtone.

A text. Lots of texts.

WHERE R U?

Oh, my God. She blinked again, her throat working but words getting lost en route to her mouth. He was here? Her heart had begun to hammer against her chest wall.

No. He was in Paris.

She texted back.

Trafalgar Square.

NO KIDDING? MORE SPECIFIC?

She really did need to tell him about his caps lock. It felt as if he were shouting. Or desperate. Was he desperate?

He was here.

He was here.

He was here and desperate and there were too many people. Why the hell hadn't she had a party at home? There would have been—what? Twenty people? Forty? Not the whole of the damned capital.

Why? So you can bah, humbug New Year's Eve, too?

I'M SORRY. REALLY. I NEED TO FIND YOU.

He needed… Tears pricked her eyes. Texting proved difficult with shaky hands.

We're next to a lion. Near the road. There's a lamppost, too. We're all here. Find us.

Please.

DO NOT MOVE

She couldn't have if she'd tried. Her legs had gone so wobbly she leaned against the lion and waited. Ignoring the countdown. Ignoring the people, as she desperately tried to see his face, the most beautiful face in this crowd.

And then he was there. In front of her. Matt and Tori and Alex and Lara faded into the ether along with the noise and the people, and the stone lion and the very, very tall Admiral Nelson. It was just Isaac. And her.

He leaned in close, his smile sheepish. 'Poppy. Thank God. I thought I'd never find you.'

She shrugged, because her shoulders were the only things she had any control over. Her heart had started its own little dance and her feet were glued to the concrete. 'Well, here I am.'

'Why the hell, for the first time in your whole damned life, did you decide to come here?' His arm slipped round her waist and even though she didn't think it was the most sensible thing to do she fell into his arms, breathing him in. Feeling his heat around her.

'I wanted to forget you.'

'And did you?'

'No. How can I forget you when you follow me and tell the whole damned crowd with that sign thingy? How did you do that, by the way?'

His gorgeous mouth turned up at the corners and she wanted, ached, longed, to kiss him. But she didn't. She listened to him instead. 'I have my ways. I told them it was an emergency.'

'Is it?'

'Absolutely.'

The noise around them pressed in, louder. 'Nearly mid-night?'

He nodded. 'Two minutes.'

Then she remembered he was supposed to be in Paris, because he didn't want to take any risks. He'd ruined her Christmas. She'd left and he hadn't tried to stop her. He'd broken her heart. 'Why are you here?'

His thumb stroked gently across her cheek, his eyes blazing with affection. Deep, solid, strong affection. 'I wanted to tell you—man, I wish we were somewhere private.'

'Tell me what?'

'That I want to try.'

'What do you mean?' Because she didn't want to jump to conclusions. Didn't want to think…anything. Hope…

The man who had an answer for everything seemed to be finding them hard to find tonight. 'I want you, Poppy. I can't sleep. I can't eat. Paris was dull. Everything is dull. Nothing's the same. I miss you. You're…a keeper. I'm sorry I ruined your Christmas. I really am. I'm an idiot. But…' He closed his eyes and tested out the words. She just knew it was the first time he'd said them. Knew he was trying to feel the shape of them, the taste. 'I love you.'

It was a big step. He'd put aside everything and come here for her. Taken a risk. Found her. Declared his love.

'Whoa. That's…that's gobsmacking.' She didn't tell him back. Not say the words and break the spell. Put her heart at risk. She didn't know if she could survive him leaving her again. And if he didn't believe in the hearts and roses of it all, then he didn't believe in her either. Because that was what she wanted. 'To be honest, it was just a fling.'

He took a step back, eyes snapping open. 'A fling? Poppy, really?'

'We haven't even had a proper date. I don't really know you that well.'

'You've known me your whole life. I was there, Poppy. The whole time. I know you more than anyone else and I love you more, too. We've had a gazillion dates—all those years, then this last month, nights in bed. Mornings. In the shower. Ice-skating. Every day I've got to know you just a little bit more. And every day I've loved you more, too.' Now his hands were on her back, stroking her, lulling her back to him. 'Besides, we live together already.'

'No, we don't. I've sold the flat, to Alex and Lara.'

'Wow—I turn my back for two minutes and you sell the place from under my feet.' His mouth was on her neck now, and goddamn if she didn't want it all over her.

'Oh? You, too? From under your feet? What was I supposed to do? Wait? You all went off and left me. I'm loosening the ties. I'm living my life instead of watching everyone live theirs. First off, I'm going on holiday. To South America.'

'Where?'

'Mexico.'

His eyebrows rose. 'That's in North America.'

'I'm going on holiday to North America.'

The sound of Big Ben's bells began to pound sonorously into the night air and the buzz of anticipation grew almost electric around them.

Ten.

Now he was taking her hands in his, facing her. Serious. Beautiful, but serious. 'You want to make it a honeymoon?'

Nine.

'What?'

Eight.

'You want to make it a honeymoon? You and me. Mexico.'

'This is a proposal? Here on New Year's Eve?'

Seven.

'Will they all just be quiet? I... Well, yes.' He looked a little surprised, but determined. 'Yes. Yes, it is. I love you, Poppy. I want to spend the rest of my life with you. I want you.'

'You're not just getting carried away by the bouquets and the bling?'

'Never. I'm carried away by you. Everything starts and ends with you. I want to wake up with you every day. God, I've missed that. I want to come home to you every night. And I want to make you happy, to give you everything you want. If you want a wedding we'll have one. A future. Our future. I don't want to spend my life in the wilderness when I know this is what I want.' Then he pressed his mouth to hers. 'I love you.'

His eyes filled with such affection, such tangible, real love, that she knew with every tiny fragment of her heart that he did. 'Oh, my God, Isaac Blair. I love you, too.'

'So is that a yes?' First time ever she'd seen hesitation and anxiety in his eyes.

'Yes! Yes! Yes!'

She was pretty sure there was a lot of cheering then, and hugging and kissing; and mixing with the snowflakes there was confetti and fireworks lighting up the sky. Somewhere, everywhere, a whole world was singing about cups of kindness and not forgetting about people you've known your whole life.

And if the celebrations weren't all for them and their future she didn't mind at all because there was a lot of kissing going on for her, anyway. And a whole lot more to come.

When she eventually opened her eyes it was to the fanfare of her friends' clapping and cheering amid brushing the now fast-falling snow from their shoulders.

Alex was the first to shake Isaac's hand. 'No leg breaking needed? Shame. But well done, anyway. I suppose I should say, welcome to the family—if you hadn't been part of it your whole life already.'

Tori was next with her generous hugs for them both. 'Oh, that's so perfect. Just perfect. Wait until Izzy hears about this—she's going to be spitting she missed it. We just knew you two were made for each other. Didn't I say so, Lara?'

'Yes, you did. Congratulations, Mr Big Kahuna and lovely Poppy.' Lara pulled her in for a hug and Poppy hung on tight. Another friend, another member of their very special family.

And Matt was there, last but not least, wrapping his old friend into a fist-pump, man-hug thing. 'Good on you. What do you reckon? Best man material?'

Alex coughed. 'Ahem? Oldest friend prerogative?'

'Now, now, boys, don't fight over me.' Isaac grinned, but his smile wasn't for anyone but Poppy.

She couldn't believe how lucky she was. From a very rocky start to the month when she'd felt as if she'd lost everything, she now had it all. They all did. And more. So much more.

It was going to be a very Happy New Year indeed.

* * * * *

*If you loved this book, make sure you catch
the rest of the incredible*
THE FLAT IN NOTTING HILL *miniseries!*

THE MORNING AFTER THE NIGHT BEFORE
by Nikki Logan
available August 2014

SLEEPING WITH THE SOLDIER
by Charlotte Phillips
available September 2014

YOUR BED OR MINE?
by Joss Wood
available October 2014

ENEMIES WITH BENEFITS
by Louisa George
available November 2014

Mills & Boon® Hardback
November 2014

ROMANCE

MEDICAL